KNOTTED LACES

EAGLES HOCKEY #2

ELISE FABER

KNOTTED LACES
BY ELISE FABER

Newsletter sign-up

KNOTTED LACES
Copyright © 2024 Elise Faber
Print ISBN-13: 978-1-63749-129-4
Ebook ISBN-13: 978-1-63749-128-7

EAGLES HOCKEY SERIES

Eagles Hockey Series (all stand alone)
Broken Laces
Lace 'em Up
Knotted Laces
Loaded Laces
Lucky Laces

PROLOGUE

I LAY on the floor between my window and my bed, arms crossed behind my head, sleep a long way away as…

I eavesdrop.

Not on my brother, though I'm barely listening to the case he's discussing with his best friend who might as well be my adopted brother because he's been around for so much of my childhood.

Not on Lex either, the aforementioned brother in all but blood, as he talks about some big time multi-country criminal case that just landed on his desk.

On—

Well, I'm eavesdropping and yet not listening to either one of the men sprawled out on the deck chairs below my open window because I'm too focused on the fact that…

Lex's partner is fucking hot.

So yeah, I'm eavesdropping like a motherfucker.

On *her*.

Straining as I search the conversation below for hear any hint of her voice.

The crisp notes of the West Coast clinging to her consonants. The contrasting lilting melody of her laugh. The confidence. The swagger. The sure way she handled a Glock at our annual Jackson target shooting competition—which she won, by the way.

Lex's partner is all I've been able to see in my dreams for the last week she's been staying at my parents' lake house.

Summer's brought her and I together—at least in my mind.

Because she's barely looked at me the entire week except to ask me to pass the salt or to say "Excuse me" as she slips by me so she can throw something in the trash.

I—on the other hand—have committed as much of her to memory as possible.

Which is how I know she smells like vanilla and jasmine.

And has freckles on the bridge of her nose.

And two earrings in her right ear—one shaped like a shell, the other like a starfish.

So yeah, summer's brought me a new obsession.

Mostly because I've already jerked off every night to Athena Phillips—or Attie, if you want to be the demonstration dummy for the taser portion of the self-defense class she teaches in her spare time, or Ats, if you want to live *without* copious amounts of electricity cascading through your body.

She's an obsession I don't think I'll be able to rid myself of any time in the near future.

Mostly because that sexy body of hers has spent the last week traipsing its way through my wet dreams.

And why I can't think of her as anything but Athena.

She's a goddess—with long, lean strength, dark, curly hair, and an ass that makes me want to get on my knees and beg the rest of the Greek gods just for a chance to kiss her feet.

"...so the report doesn't show anything unusual," she's telling my brother on a sigh.

"Hmm," my brother says. "And what about the information from..."

I tune out again, not refocusing until I hear her voice.

"Nothing. It's all clean and…"

As she talks, I think about the way she smiled at me at dinner —after offering me the bowl of mashed potatoes. Is that progress? Or just more of the same?

"So, I don't know." She sighs. "It's a tangle for sure."

"Don't sound so upset," Lex rumbles, tone teasing. "You know you love nothing more than a challenge."

I commit that piece of information to memory, doubly so when she laughs, when I hear that single glimpse of soft amongst strong and capable and badass and know that Lex's teasing is filled with truth.

They continue to talk as I add that to my mental list of things I've learned about Athena Phillips.

Bad ass FBI agent.

Great shot.

Competitive.

Removed.

Quiet and set apart unless she's like this—with Lex at her side.

Family seems to be a mystery to her.

And I'm desperate to know why.

Fucking *obsessed*.

"Well," Lex says, snapping me out of my thoughts. "I'm going to head off to bed."

"Me too," my brother says.

There's the noise of chairs scraping and footsteps on the porch and—

"I'll catch up with you guys in the morning," Athena says. "I just want to enjoy the night for a bit longer."

There's something wistful about the statement and I still, wanting to know why.

Wanting to know everything about her.

Maybe that's why I listen to them exchange good nights and wait for their footsteps to move inside, up the stairs, to disappear into their respective bedrooms. Maybe it's why when Athena doesn't come inside, I slip out of my room and into the kitchen, peering out through the wide window behind the sink and seeing her sitting in the chair, head tilted up toward the sky, curls flowing down her back in a sweep of dark waves.

I stare, soaking her in.

And I don't know if it's because she's in law enforcement and her instincts are honed—or just because I'm standing there like a creeper, staring at her from the shadows of the kitchen—but eventually she spins around.

I freeze as our eyes connect.

My heart launches itself against my rib cage as she pushes up out of the chair, starts for the door to the kitchen, and I scramble, searching for anything that won't make me look like a fucking creep…

And have the feeling I fail as she walks through the door and I'm still standing there like a fucking creeper.

"Cam," she murmurs in greeting.

"Athena," I manage back.

Her brows flick up, eyes promising retribution.

"Sorry," I mutter, wrapping my fingers around a glass. "Uh, I meant, Ats," I amend. I hold up the cup. "I…uh…just needed some water and a snack."

Right on cue, my stomach growls.

Thank you, always hungry body.

Her face relaxes and she leans a hip against the counter, mouth curving up slightly at the edges. "You've had a couple of long days."

Training. Getting ready for the season. Hitting the local rink and the gym and the trails around the house. I've got training camp in a couple of weeks and if it goes well, I might make the roster this season.

Not the AHL.

But The Show.

The big leagues. Playing professional hockey in front of tens of thousands of people.

My fucking dream.

"Anything really important is worth putting in the hard work," I say softly.

Her head tilts to the side, those curls bouncing behind her like a silken cloud and she smiles outright this time.

The impact is like a punch to my solar plexus.

And it loosens my tongue.

"You're beautiful," I blurt.

Her smile fades, is wiped away almost comically fast, and—Christ—but the emotions that take its places are like rubbing sandpaper over my naked skin. "Cam," she begins.

"I...just mean it objectively speaking," I blather. "You're beautiful like a painting's beautiful, or like...a tree."

The only positive thing about that statement is that she smiles again.

"I—"

She pushes off the counter, reaches toward the cookie jar, and pulls out a handful of apple oat cookies—one of my mom's specialties.

And my favorite.

A fact that sends my heart lurching against my ribs again.

"Eat, drink, and sleep," she says softly as she presses them into my hand.

"I—"

But before I can formulate anything else—like a complete fucking thought or a compliment that's not comparing her to a fucking *tree*—she's gone…

I stand there and listen to her footsteps disappear upstairs.

Then I eat the cookies, drink a glass of water, and jerk off to the vision of that small smile, the softness in her eyes, and…dark curls bouncing as she walks away from me.

And, in the morning, I realize I'm lucky to have even that much.

Because, in the morning…
She's gone.

CHAPTER ONE

Cam, Present Day

THE CROWD BOOS, but I don't give a fuck.

That's par for the course in professional hockey.

And since we're the away team tonight, the jeers from the Grizzlies fans mean we're doing something right.

I grunt as I take the elbow to the back of the head, but don't give up the puck.

Instead, I focus, ignore the pain that radiates down my neck, tensing my core, digging my skates into the ice, and look for my teammate.

Rome cuts hard toward me, exactly like we planned, freeing up space, moving along the play we drew up, giving…

King the lane.

Before I can take advantage of that, my face is all but slammed into the boards, another fucker from the Grizzlies coming in hot. He's big as shit with a long, scraggly beard.

Connor Smith.

Or Smitty, as he's colloquially know to the hockey world at large.

Nice guy. *Funny* guy.

But pain in the fucking ass to play against.

Another shove has me eating glass, but I've delayed long enough. "Fuck," I grit, shoving back and flicking my stick, sending the puck flying toward the center of the ice.

King sweeps it up, drives toward the goal, and—

The crowd roars in happiness as he's slashed hard and loses the puck. In a flash, the play swings the other way, the Grizzlies taking control and sprinting toward our end of the ice.

And just that quickly we're on defense, chasing down the other team, hauling ass to protect our goalie.

Digging in.

Not giving up.

The entire game is a grind, spending sixty minutes trying to eke out a win, something we don't quite manage in the end.

Which means that the mood amongst my teammates is shit as we exit the ice and move down the hall to the locker room. It's just a game, but it's our livelihood and we get paid the big bucks to win—literally, since the Eagles gave me my first big seven-figure contract. So, losing in any capacity is unacceptable, but most especially in the playoffs.

Expected.

But still not good enough.

Especially when the play I came up with resulted in the goal that cost us the game and put us down in the series.

Cursing under my breath, I drop my helmet into the bin the equipment guys have wheeled in to the center of the locker room and sink down onto the bench so I can change out of the rest of my gear. The space is quiet, most everyone pissed off and sulky like the man-children we are. It's frustrating, especially after working our asses off, even more so when it means that we're going to have to battle even harder.

At least we're close enough to Oakland that we can drive ourselves home and I don't have to wait for my teammates so we can board a fucking bus or plane.

King drops down next to me with a sigh. "Tough one," he

grumbles as he rips his jersey over his head, sending it sailing across the room and into another bin.

"Tough one," Pat, resident asshole on the team, sneers. "Fucking brilliant, King Bang."

Duncan, the team's manwhore—who's never met a woman, or man for that matter, he isn't interested in fucking—chuckles like the dumbass he is. And, as always, he has to chime in. Today it's with the gem, "Whatever gave you that idea?"

I roll my eyes, start yanking at my skate laces.

King just shakes his head and tears at the Velcro on his shoulder pads.

Rome, our captain, just grunts in response, ignoring both Tweedledee and Tweedledum and the smirk they exchange.

I shove down the frustration and the disappointment, the feeling that the loss is my fault. I know shit happens, that it was all of us out there on the ice, so it's not solely my fault, same as I know we'll regroup and keep moving forward—mostly because we've found a way to work together over the last months to cinch the top spot in our division.

Last place in the league to roaring into the playoffs.

Unfortunately, that momentum seems to have come to a screeching halt.

Same as the unity we cobbled together in the locker room is beginning to unravel.

Pat laughs like Duncan is the most hysterical comedian in the world.

Unity? What fucking unity?

We have those two idiots. Along with hotheaded Kane, Lazy Matt, Asshole Anthony. All of whom are looking around for someone to blame who's not themselves.

Ugh.

Sometimes my job sucks.

Especially when *I* fuck up and they *should* blame me and—

King exhales, nudges his knee against mine. "Shake it off, yeah?"

"I'm good," I mutter, but I know *he* knows it's bullshit. Thankfully, though, he doesn't call me on it further—just shoots me a look and continues getting changed.

"It's one game, boys," Rome says, taking off his frustrated player hat and replacing it with his captain one. Focused. Steady. *Good.* That's Rome. "There are two more in the series," he adds. "So there's plenty of time to knock 'em out." He tears off and tosses his own jersey in the bin. "We just need to calm down and stay focused, to keep playing our system and grinding it out."

Except the Grizzlies are now up three games to two.

And if they win one more, our Cinderella season—last place to first, and a real contender for the Cup—is over.

I exhale, trying to take Rome's words to heart.

He's right. We have time.

We just need to chill. To focus and play our game and keep moving forward.

But all of his calm confidence still makes me want to smack my friend. He's self-assured. He doesn't waver. He just puts his head down and keeps driving toward his goals. Exactly the same way the Eagles' owner and Rome's future father-in-law, Jean-Michel Dubois, does.

Probably why they get along so well…

And why Jean-Michel didn't have Rome killed for daring to touch his daughter.

Or propose to her.

Or move in with her before they officially tied the knot.

The tension in my shoulders loosens.

I bet *that* was a fun conversation.

Grumpy billionaire with a decidedly scary edge having to face the fact that his baby girl is all grown up.

Thank God Rome has all that calm confidence—he can walk into the dragon's den and come out unscathed.

Now, if only I can channel some of that.

And stop thinking about that fucking play.

I'm still struggling with that as Cassie, who works in Game

Day Operations (or basically, who works in the gets-to-boss-us-around-most-of-the-time-and-we-just-shut-up-and-follow-her-lead department), pops her head in through the door. "Media coming in."

Not a question.

Just…a heads up wrapped around an order.

Give good sound bites we can chop up and use on social media, don't flash anyone your junk, and absolutely no fucking fist fights that can be caught on camera.

The last, one would think is hyperbole.

With this team?

Not so much.

The Eagles and scuffles in the locker room are synonymous. Pat and Duncan. Pat and Asshole Anthony. Pat and hothead Kane. Pat and Lazy as shit Matt. Pat and Duncan again.

For a while, I swear my parents didn't see a single clip of my team actually playing hockey.

It was all pushing and shoving, fists connecting, bleeped curses and fucking *Pat*.

And, as fate would fucking have it, the one game my parents have made it to in a while is tonight's.

The one where we lost.

Because of me.

Cool. Cool.

A fist fight in the locker room that gets splashed all over social media would be the cherry on top of that.

Sighing, I slap on a hat to cover my helmet hair, shove down my whiny baby bullshit, and turn my focus to the press core who are walking into the room, cameras on shoulders, phone with recording apps open already pointed in our directions.

I give my sound bite.

Take my shower.

Pull on my street clothes.

And then I'm nodding my goodbyes to King and Rome, both

of whom are still stuck talking to the press, before slipping out into the hall and heading for my car.

My phone buzzes.

MOM: We're headed back to your house, honey. Will have your post-game snack ready for you.

That makes me feel like something other than a failure (for the record, hungry because my mom is a great cook)…and I hurry to the parking lot.

It's been ages since she's made me a recovery meal but I know it'll be right in line with my diet and fucking delicious and that it will *absolutely* be the best thing to happen today.

So, I don't waste any time in driving home, in parking in the garage, in grabbing my stuff and hustling my ass into the house.

Apples and cinnamon—my favorite combination on the planet—greet me before I even turn the corner into the kitchen. It's that delicious smell that has me belatedly recognizing there are voices echoing into the hall, that has me not processing that my house is full of people until I actually step into the brightly lit space.

"Surprise!" they shout.

My brothers—all six of them (biological and otherwise)—and my sister (not biologically related, but still my sister) are filling up the room.

And their spouses.

And their kids—half of whom are passed out in arms or on my couches, while the other half are running around like the tiny terrors they are.

I'm engulfed in hugs and hellos and conversations for several minutes before everyone begins to peel off, my mom shoves an apple-cinnamon oat cookie into my hand, and I see there's someone else in the room who I missed.

Athena, or Ats as she prefers to go by, is here, hanging back as usual—a part of the festivities but also separate—as she stands in my kitchen talking to my brothers.

Everything in me goes still.

Because *Athena*, as she *hates* to go by, is looking like the goddess she is, her curls flowing around her shoulders, an Eagles jersey clinging to her delicious body.

She laughs at something Lex says as she nibbles on an apple oat cookie.

And I want to drop to my knees in front of her and beg her to see me.

Unfortunately, that will never be.

I've had a decade to come to terms with that fact.

A decade to understand that she won't ever be mine.

So, I pull it together, tuck down the draw I always feel when she's near, but when she turns…

I lose all semblance of focus as my brain processes what's on the back of her jersey.

It's my name. My number.

Mine.

Only…not.

Because she's in love with my brother.

CHAPTER TWO

Athena

THE KIDDOS ARE SPRAWLED out on blowup mattresses in the living room, their limbs tangled with their cousins', blankets printed with brightly patterned children's television show characters tucked in around their little bodies.

It's a beautiful sight, one that tugs at even my hardened-to-ice heart.

Innocent and loved and protected.

Unlike what I had—

I clamp my teeth together, nearly taking off my own finger as I shove one of Martha's homemade oat cookies into my mouth.

Oat and cookie.

Those things don't sound like they should go together and taste like anything but sawdust, but Martha Jackson—matriarch of this family of blood and friendship—is a fantastic cook.

It's why I keep visiting them.

Not the *only* reason, of course—though it definitely drew me in the door in the first place and made it so I didn't complain all that much when Lex initially dragged me along on a Jackson family vacation almost a decade ago.

He's a sneaky bastard who had primed the dragging by bringing cinnamon rolls into the break room at work—cinnamon rolls that disappeared faster than our former boss during a team building exercise.

Ooey, gooey, and deliciously buttery. Add in being topped with a thick orange-zest and cream cheese frosting and…

Well, there's a reason Martha gives me a freezer full of them every Christmas.

And why I always send her for a full body spa day in return.

I set the cookie down and take a swig of my beer, trying to focus on cinnamon rolls and apple oat cookies.

Which is…moderately successful.

Mostly because the past is a clingy bitch. Being here. On the West Coast. In the Bay Area…

It brings back long-buried enemies.

This is where I grew up.

Before we swapped coasts, and before things got really bad there…they were bad *here*.

But even with that in my head, I know needed this change, needed the chance to work on this case, and as much as I miss the day-to-day with Lex—we were partners in the FBI together for ten years, for God's sake—it's good to have a fresh start.

My life here is long over.

My demons are back East.

Along with Lex.

Because now he has Frankie. Hell, *all* the Jacksons on the East Coast are matched up and blissfully happy and…

That's not my future.

Sighing, I clench my back teeth together and deliberately pick up my cookie, taking small bites until it's gone, until I'm focused on anything that isn't…

Well, that isn't *my* family. My past. And…what I won't ever have.

Luckily, with the Jacksons around, that's not all that hard.

Six brothers (though Lex isn't technically a bio-relative, he's more like me—swept into the fold and not let go). A movie star adopted sister. Five daughters by marriage and a gaggle of kids.

Which means there's always something interesting happening.

Like Cam—who's grown into his adult body and is somehow sporting even more muscles since the last time I saw him— getting noogies from Carter. And then Chance. And Connor. And Caleb. And…Lex, who can't resist joining in.

Cam takes the teasing good-naturedly for a few minutes then bats them away, "Well at least *I* can actually lift more than five pounds in the gym." He pats Lex's flat stomach, pokes at Carter's side. "You guys have been packing the pounds ever since you got hitched—"

Lex growls and I smother a smile, knowing he's sensitive about his not-so-six-pack since he hooked up with Frankie. The funny part is that she owns a health store, so it should be easy. Unfortunately for Lex, she's also a great cook, along with Martha and Sophie, *and* all the Jackson daughters by marriage. None of which is easy on the waistline.

It's only because of my recent transfer to the Oakland office that I've managed to continue to fit into my jeans.

But I'm not above buying a size up either.

"You're dead," Lex mutters, taking a step toward Cam.

Who, grinning, darts away, hustling across the kitchen to Martha. He wraps his arms around her from behind. "Save me, Mom!"

She tilts her head back and lifts on tiptoe to press a kiss to his stubble-covered cheek. "I love you."

My heart pulses—because it's sweet and heartfelt and it's the truth. And also because Martha barely gets the words out before I realize that Chance has sneaked up behind Cam. With a growl, he scoops his littlest brother up like a sack of potatoes and starts hauling him from the room.

"Ack!" Cam grunts, arms and legs flying. "*Chance!*"

"Nice try, bubby," Martha says, moving between the flying

limbs with all the experience of a mom of eight. She pats him on the cheek. "But you created this monster, so now you get to pay the piper—"

With another grunt, Cam executes a move that has my law enforcement heart lurching in my chest—because it's fucking impressive and shows exactly how strong the youngest Jackson brother has gotten.

And handsome.

That smirk. The stubble. The gorgeous hazel eyes. The ass that any woman would be lucky enough to grab on to as he plunged deep and hard and—

What the actual fuck?

I nearly bite my fingers off again.

The cookie in my mouth turns to sawdust.

Was I actually thinking about little Cam Jackson like—

My stomach starts churning.

Nope. Cam is little *Cam*. Abjectly handsome and good-looking like all the Jacksons, but definitely not sexy, definitely not in possession of a gorgeous ass I get a glimpse of as he wrestles with Lex—

Holy hell.

His ass is just an ass.

That's it.

And that's why I turn away from the sight of the youngest Jackson, searching out my coat and purse—it's just an ass. One that has no effect on me.

Nope.

No effect whatsoever.

"You okay, honey?"

I still, my arms halfway into my jacket, and look up at the only woman who's ever called me *honey*. "Yeah, Martha," I tell her. "I just have an early morning tomorrow."

"Early morning on vacation?"

I still at the voice that trails like fingers down my spine and turn to see Cam, looking a little disheveled from his scuffle with his brothers, but whole as he strides toward us. His smile is sexy and confident and—

Stop.

"Early morning at work," I quietly correct. "Not vacation."

His brows drag together. "Work?" He glances over his shoulder at Lex. "Are you guys working a case?"

"Didn't I tell you, baby?" Martha says, moving toward him and looping her arm around his waist. "Ats"—because Martha always calls me by my nickname of choice, because *of course* she does—"transferred to the Oakland office a couple of months ago."

Now his brows shoot up. "Months?"

I don't miss the hint of accusation in his tone or in his gorgeous Jackson-hazel eyes—nor the confusion because if anyone else in this family I've been folded into had moved to the same city as the team he plays for, he would know about it.

But…I'm me.

I keep my distance. It's the only way I know how to live.

"I'm just now getting settled in," I prevaricate, trying to shove down another blip of guilt. "I had a case I was wrapping up that required a lot of travel and then the move and—"

The accusation doesn't disappear like I hope.

In fact, it seems to grow.

As does the guilt.

You'll never be part of them. Not really.

The voice in my mind slices deep and it takes everything in me to not close my eyes, to not hold myself still, to not wait until the pain fades. Instead, I just keep my shields in place and press on. "I'm settled in now, though, so the timing worked out perfectly when your mom invited me to watch the game and surprise you tonight. I got to see you play some hockey in person—which was impressive by the way—*and* I got baked goods. Win-win."

He frowns, but I don't acknowledge it.

Noise increases from the kitchen, drawing Martha's focus.

"Night," I tell her. "Thanks for the yummy food." I move in and hug her tight before she shooing her away so she can head into the kitchen and negotiate a truce between Carter and Caleb.

My lips curl up at the edges.

The Jackson brothers.

Chaos personified.

Always.

But when I turn to Cam any amusement in my belly fades.

"Thanks for letting us invade your house," I say softly.

He studies me for a blip too long and I can't miss the hurt in his eyes.

Shit.

I fucked up. I should have told him and—

His face clears as he hitches a thumb over his shoulder. His smile is normal, and relief floods my insides. I can't bear to hurt him, can't bear to hurt *any* of them.

"You're welcome anytime," he says, hugging me briefly and I feel that blip in my stomach again, as though I'm riding a roller coaster, cresting the first rise just before the big drop, waiting for the rest of the cars to catch up before we fly. "As if I ever had a choice with this crew."

"True. There's no stopping a Jackson invasion," I agree, ignoring that rollercoaster inside me even as I step back and grin at him. My heart is pounding, and my palms are sweaty.

What the fuck is wrong with me?

He leans back against the wall and crosses his arms, causing the muscles beneath his short-sleeved shirt to stand out sharply in relief. "I accepted that long ago," he says lightly.

My body drifts towards his and the slightly spicy scent of him fills my senses.

I want to lean closer.

To inhale deeply.

To touch and kiss and—

Seriously.

What. The. *Fuck?*

I straighten and panic has my hands shaking as I zip up my jacket. "Well, I, um—" I clear my throat. "I need to head out. I'll see ya around." I settle my purse on my shoulder and start for the door, not realizing he's followed me until he reaches past me and opens the wooden panel.

I still, feeling...

Nope.

Not feeling *anything.*

"You know how to get home?" he asks quietly.

"Yup," I say tartly as I step out onto the porch. "New to the area, but not new to Google Maps."

"Noted." He lifts his palms, mouth curved, clearly picking up on my tone. But one has to be careful with these Jacksons. Give them an inch and pretty soon you're part of a family of more than twenty nosy nellies.

Speaking of which, I need to go.

But something keeps my feet glued to the concrete of the porch. "You played good tonight," I say then freeze when something crosses his face. Something like—

Pain.

Cam Jackson is in pain.

"What is it?" I ask, heart kicking against my rib cage. "Did you get hurt in the game?"

Just that quickly, the emotion is gone, tucked away, shoved down, and...fuck, if that doesn't make me want to rage against the world. He shouldn't have to bury his emotions, shouldn't have to hide.

Not Cam.

He's *good.*

Which might be why I do something stupid.

Something that sends me down a slippery slope of inevitability.

It's why—instead of leaving—I close the distance between us and...

Hug him tightly.

CHAPTER THREE

Cam

"MEOW!"

I grunt when the cat lands on my stomach and immediately starts making biscuits, ignoring the fact that I was trying to get up off the floor. She plunks down, taking her time to make herself comfortable, clearly not giving a fuck about anything other than finding a place to sleep.

A place that's inconvenient for me, so it's better for her.

"Joan," I grumble, giving in to the inevitable and lowering myself back to the floor.

At least I have an actual pillow for my head—that's a perk that comes from entertaining a gaggle of rescue kittens that Chrissy, Rome's girlfriend, Jean-Michel's daughter—and the owner of a local cat charity—is currently housing.

Joan turns her head and fixes me with a stern stare. "*Meow,*" she warns.

"Joan of *Freaking* Arc," I correct quickly.

"Meow," she says, pleased and closes her eyes, purrs vibrating through her furry body.

"If, six months ago, I thought she'd be doing anything but

hissing at everyone and trying to go full Assault Cat, I'd be lying," Chrissy says.

I turn my head, careful not to disturb the warrior queen of cats and glance over at Rome's girlfriend, my lips tugging up at the sight of her sprawled out like I am and covered nearly head to toe in sleeping kittens. Then I return my focus to my own bundle of fur. I dare to slowly reach out and gently scratch the top of Joan's head. She rumbles a bit in warning—because she used to be that surly, assault cat—but tolerates my indiscretion. "She just needed a persistent hockey player to melt that icy exterior," I declare.

An icy exterior that another woman in my life has.

One who is prickly and great at slamming down frosty, impenetrable walls and didn't even tell me she moved twenty-five hundred miles across the country to put down roots in my city.

Ats has always been distant, untouchable, and not for me.

Because she looks at Lex like he's her world—or *had* anyway, before he fell for Frankie, and she moved across the country, and—

She started doing things like hugging me and whispering, *"You're good, Cam. So damned good. I hope you know that."*

For a second last night I thought maybe I was wrong. Maybe I misread all of it, the years, the closeness, the soft smiles she had for my brother.

But then Lex opened the door, his fingers wrapped around Frankie's, both of them smiling and laughing, and…

Everything changed.

Ats closed down, and pulled back, her face a mask, her arms tense at her side. Her goodnight to us all had been terse before she was retreating, the soft curves that had made every nerve in my body stand up in rigid attention gone as she hurried down my front walkway, got in her car, and left.

"Grr," Joan rumbles in displeasure.

"You like it," I counter and keep scratching.

A narrow-eyed glare but she deigns to allow me to continue touching her.

"See?" I press.

She makes a halfhearted attempt at swatting at me but settles in and closes her eyes again.

Chrissy giggles. "Who would have thought hot"—she gives me a teasing wink—"*and* persistent hockey players could be felled by grumpy felines?"

"You?"

We both turn our heads at the sound of Rome's teasing voice, watch as he prowls into the room, expertly navigating cat toys and water dishes and litter boxes until he reaches Chrissy's side.

"That's true," she says lightly, lifting her head slightly, instinctively knowing what he's going to do next—bend down and kiss her.

I feel that in my gut, feel it settle right alongside the jealousy that's been eating at my soul.

My parents and their happy marriage mean there's much to live up to. And my siblings have taken on the mantle. First, my sister, Soph, met Rob. And then my brothers fell one by one by one—Chance and Carter, Caleb and Connor, and Lex. Even *Lex*—self-proclaimed bachelor who had no interest in settling down—*ever*—had met his match.

And Rome with the fucking owner's daughter.

And King with Jean-Michel's all-but adopted one.

And me…

Who's in love with a woman who's in love with my brother, but who is also too good of a person to try to interfere in a relationship that makes him happy, so she moved across the country and—

I bite back a sigh, know I need to get over this.

Athena is a woman who barely looks at me, who hardly acknowledges my presence, who—

Hugged me for once.

Didn't just accept the affection that my family and I doled out, but actually *initiated* the move.

Unfathomable.

Maybe it's the California air turning hard-assed Ats into a hippie extraordinaire, and now Free Love and Athena Phillips go hand in hand.

Right.

That's likely.

I must have moved or breathed wrong or laughed silently at my dumbass internal dialogue because Joan rumbles her displeasure at me. "Chill, little battle cat," I mutter, carefully scratching her beneath her fuzzy chin. "I'll try to breathe less."

Rome chuckles as he sprawls on the floor next to his woman, not flinching when the movement rouses some of the kittens and they start to claw their way up his body. I wince in solidarity, having spent most of the evening playing pin cushion to their tiny, needle-like claws, but Rome doesn't seem to notice—

Except when one crawls up the insides of his thigh.

"Easy, little fluffball" he tells the kitten, "I still need those parts."

I huff out a laugh—a full one this time without worry of retribution because Joan of Freaking Arc has realized her favorite person is in the room and has decided to stop using me as a cat perch. She strolls over to Rome, her tail flicking in displeasure at the kittens, but still showing remarkable patience as they twine themselves around her legs and try to pounce on her and want to curl up next to her when she settles on Rome's chest.

Prickly, but patient. Grumpy but kind.

Kind of like another perplexing female in my life.

And…am I obsessed?

Unfortunately, yes. I've been that way for almost a decade.

Plus, rehashing a hug—yes, I'm aware of how pathetic that makes me—is so much better than rehashing the game the day before.

Sighing silently, I push up to sitting, grimacing at the

pinpricks from the kittens' claws in my sweats, but knowing that it's part of being here. Part of hanging out with people I care about and helping them for a few hours (since Rome had to step out and deal with a crisis with one of his former teammates—babysitting because one of their other kids needed to go to the hospital).

Same as I know it's win-win, really.

Because it also gave me an excuse to escape some of the chaos at my house.

I love it, love my family. But they're a lot, and my place is full to the brim of my siblings and their kids and my parents for the next two days—all of whom are blissfully happy.

All of whom remind me of exactly what I *don't* have.

"How's Roxie?" I ask quietly.

Rome sighs. "Broke both bones in her arm, but totally a champ." He chuckles and endures the wrath of Jane of Freaking Arc swiping out a paw. "Brit and Stefan, on the other hand, are wrecks."

"It's different when it's your kid—or at least that's what my parents say."

"I can only imagine," Chrissy says softly, settling a hand on her belly.

My stomach knots and for a second, my mind starts to unravel.

Pain. And fear. The knowledge that I can't do anything different, can't be better, can't change the facts—all welling up and threatening to pull me from this moment.

Enough.

I just shove those thoughts down, and cling to the tell. This isn't about me. It's about them, about Chrissy. And if I've learned anything from my mom it's to *never*—fucking *never*—ask a woman if she's pregnant.

So if Chrissy *is* touching her belly because there's a baby on the way…

Well, I'll be happy for her and Rome.

I'll make certain of that.

Even if it kills me.

Grinding my teeth together, I lock that away, push to my feet, and start for the hall. "Speaking of parents," I tell them. "I'd better get home."

Rome grins. "If you need another breather, I'm sure that Chrissy will have some litter boxes to scoop."

I grin back. "You'll need to pay me more than in free baked goods from Molly's for that."

"*Meow!*"

I glance over at Rome, who's dislodged a very unhappy Joan of Freaking Arc and the gaggle of kittens. Our eyes meet. "I'll walk you out," he says, tone brokering no argument.

For Christ's sake.

"I know the way." I start for the door.

"I'll *walk* you out."

Great. I barely hold back my scowl.

"I'm fine," I mutter the moment we walk through the front door.

"*Fine* means beating yourself up for last night?" he counters, closing the wooden panel behind us.

I head for my car. "It was my play. It cost us a goal. And that was the difference in the game last night." I shrug as I bleep the locks. "You can't explain that away with bad hockey luck, Cap."

Rome's quiet as I settle into the car, which I'm fucking grateful for.

I'll get over my frustration.

I always do. Being the youngest Jackson means that I've had plenty of time to play comparison games and come up short of my successful older siblings.

"I'll be grumpy about it for a few days," I say, trying to diffuse his obvious concern. "But I'll go back to the drawing board and come up with something better."

Because I always do.

He catches the door before I can close it, his gaze clashing with mine.

"I'll give you this one," he says quietly, and I barely hold back my sigh of relief. "But the team is a family, Cam—or we're going to make it one, anyway." His fingers flex. "And I *know* there's something else going on in the big, juicy brain of yours. So, if you think I'm going to let you drown in that bullshit tearing you apart, you've lost your mind."

He gives the door a shove, closing it firmly before he turns for the house and leaves me to my drive home.

But my moment of relief is just that.

A moment.

Because, unfortunately, he's right.

There *is* more going on.

I've been treading water for months now.

It's just…my arms and legs are tired and my head's about to slip beneath the water for the final time.

CHAPTER FOUR

Athena

A COUPLE of days after watching Cam's game with the rest of the Jacksons, I exhale and squeeze the Glock's trigger, the kickback from the handgun barely registering.

Natural.

Normal.

Just…another day at the shooting range.

Another exhale and then I'm firing again, concentrating hard, making sure all of my shots are hitting the biggest target—the torso. Of course, it's always easier to hit a paper target than a real person—and not just because a person moves. There's something terrible about bullets hitting flesh, the blood, the devastation that comes after for everyone.

I haven't been in many firefights, but…

The aftermath is something that clings to the quiet moments, to the darkness in the middle of the night, when sleep eludes me and the world seems like a very scary face.

I got into this line of work to find control, to conquer the horrible shit that haunted my childhood.

It both worked and didn't.

The stuff that used to scare me doesn't—I can protect myself, can be calm and levelheaded in a wide variety of tense situations. But I also know more about the world, the darkness that civilians can't even fathom, and—

In some ways, it's even scarier.

I empty the last of the bullets from the magazine then set the gun down and hit the button to bring the target over to my end of the lane.

"Impressive."

I'd already sensed Lex's presence behind me, so I don't react other than to turn around and lean back against the counter. "Thought you were heading to the airport."

He and the other Jacksons are heading out today. The kids need to get back to school and the shops that Misty and Frankie own in the quiet town of Stoneybrook need to be reopened. And Lex, Chance, and Carter all have open cases.

Plus, they want to be out of Cam's hair before his next playoff game tonight *and* home from the airport and settled so they can watch the match up on TV.

But Lex doesn't address any of that.

He just scowls and crosses his arms. "You done with this shit?"

I match his energy—because sometimes you just have to. "*Shit* meaning a promotion?"

His scowl deepens. "*Shit* meaning leaving your support system and running to the other side of the country because a case went bad."

I still.

But not for long because I don't let anyone push me around, not even Lex. "It's not exactly leaving my *support system*"—I do air quotes—"when the Jacksons invade on the regular because Cam's here."

Of course, if I could have continued to work this case anywhere—fucking *anywhere*—else it wouldn't have been here, something I know that *Lex* knows given how he's looking at me.

It's soft.

Gentle.

And my stomach starts churning. "Don't," I warn.

"Shit went bad, Ats," he says. "It happens."

It happens.

"He's not an *it*," I whisper.

"No," Lex agrees. "He wasn't.

"Tommy died and he did it—" I press my lips together because I can't give voice to the rest of it.

Unfortunately, Lex knows this part too. "Saving you."

I clench my teeth so tightly that a bolt of pain shoots through my jaw. "It's part of the job," I hedge.

"Still leaves a scar."

A little boy without a father. A wife made a widow.

For *me*.

What was the fucking point? Saving a single, childless cat lady—not that I'm home enough to actually have a cat again—saving a woman who grew up in a shithole with asshole parents and leaving his family—

Enough.

I lift my chin. "You're going to miss your flight."

Lex sighs. "You've always been a stubborn fuck, haven't you?"

Thank God. He's going to let this go.

"Takes one to know one," I remind him.

His mouth kicks up. "And look where I am now."

That strikes as deeply as the bullets I'd been shooting. Because my grumpy partner is changed, is better, is in *love*.

He waves a hand at himself. "Don't you want a piece of this?"

"No thanks," I mutter. "Never have. Never will. Even though you made that move one time."

"Asshole." He slugs me. "I was an idiot recruit. And I was drunk."

"That explains the sloppy ass kiss."

"*Really* an asshole." He bumps his shoulder against mine. "And you know what I mean. Don't you want more? Don't you want something that's not just the job?"

"I already have it," I tell him honestly. "I have you, and you gave me the Jacksons, and you know what you all mean to me."

That's about as gooey as I ever get.

Something he knows because he goes soft again.

Big, tough Lex Blackwell is a softie—it's a side few people ever get to see.

"Speaking of the Jacksons," he says. "What was going on with you and Cam on the porch?"

Nothing.

Absolutely *nothing.*

The urge to blurt that out is strong…and troublesome.

I ignore it.

Then tell the truth—also ignoring that my words are only a small semblance of it. "He was upset about the game and needed a hug and some encouragement." I wrinkle my nose in disgust, though my heart's pounding in my chest.

"*You* willingly hugged someone?" Lex asks incredulously.

I scowl. "I hug."

He snorts.

Just not very often.

"And you know nothing's going on," I snap, "even before you tried with that fishing expedition."

His mouth kicks up. "A big brother has to try."

That has my heart rolling over in my chest for a whole other reason. "Lex," I whisper.

"I know," he mutters. "Just deal with the fact that I'm in your life and I know that you're hurting right now. But you can't keep running. Take it from me. That shit always catches up to you."

My lungs hitch. "You know I'm not one to settle down."

"No."

I frown.

"I *don't* know that."

"Lex."

"But I *do* know that you're too fucking scared to step out from behind those icy walls you erected around yourself."

Ouch.

I mean, he's not wrong, but—

Ouch.

"I love you, Ats," he said and that hurts too, albeit in a completely different way. "But I don't get what you're doing with your life."

I try on anger because I can't handle all the rest of it. Too many emotions. Too many feelings. Too much risk of the ice around my insides melting. "It's none of your business what I do with my fucking life."

He exhales, disappointment in his eyes. "That's what you don't get."

"What?"

"You're family," he says, pulling me into a hug and, hell, the man gives good hug. "You'll understand what that really means at some point." He sighs and drops his arms. "I just hope you'll finally see what's in front of your face before it's too late."

That ricochets through my head, stealing my words, my thoughts—

Or maybe *directing* them.

Toward someone I can't think about.

Not that way.

Not now.

Not *ever.*

He steps back when I don't say anything.

He just doesn't know *I* can't say anything.

"I'll text you when we're all settled back in Stoneybrook."

"Okay," I whisper, his words jumbling my thoughts, his hug an acute reminder of all I'm missing. "Safe flight."

A nod, and he's gone.

You're family.

You'll understand what that really means at some point.

I just hope you'll finally see what's in front of your face before it's too late

He doesn't get it.

I *do* understand. I lived the opposite for long enough to know exactly how precious good family is.

Just like I lived long enough to know that it's not something I can ever have.

————

LEX TEXTS me later that day, telling me everyone has arrived safe, and as much as I wanted to avoid the contact and pull back I don't.

I owe him that much—owe him *so* much more.

Plus, I can't risk cutting off my supply of baked goods, so I need to keep Frankie and Martha happy and that means I can't piss off one of their adopted kids.

Who am I kidding?

I need to keep Martha and Frankie happy because I can't stand for them to wake up one day and look at me like—

Well, like my mom used to look at me.

"Ugh," I mutter, slamming my laptop closed and walking into the kitchen. I need a beer, to throw one of the cinnamon rolls in my freezer into the air fryer, and to go to bed.

But that doesn't happen.

Oh, I get my cinnamon roll and my beer.

But I don't go to bed.

Instead, I turn on the TV and…

I watch the Eagles win their playoff game.

And I worry that I've already begun to see what's in front of me.

CHAPTER FIVE

Cam

WE WON.

Barely.

But we sneaked out the win and I wasn't the cause of anything that directly led to our team getting scored on.

Of course I also didn't do anything that helped the Eagles win.

Which is why Coach calls me into his office to talk before media.

To talk being code for being torn to pieces.

So now I'm grinding my back teeth together, sitting in the chair in front of his desk in sweaty undergarments, and listening to a lecture on protecting the puck.

And getting my fucking head in the game.

And pulling my fucking weight if I want to stay on the fucking roster.

"…I fucking mean it, Cam," he screams, spittle flying across the air to land in gross droplets on top of his desk and the plethora of papers and the tablet he's been shoving in my face. "You need to figure out what the fuck is going on in that big brain of yours and fix it. The team needs you and you're not doing enough."

Not enough. *Not enough.*

Right.

Exactly what I want to hear after my doctor's appointment this morning—something I squeezed in between morning skate and coming to the arena for warmups, hoping that this time it might be different news, that something might have changed. But it's the fucking same. It's *been* the fucking same for the last year and—

"So get your fucking head out of your fucking ass and do fucking *something* out there on the ice. Or you're fucking gone come next season, Cam. I fucking *mean* it."

Normally, I'd be amused by the sheer number of f-bombs that Coach has managed to insert into this conversation.

But...

I'm really not in the *fucking*—no pun intended—mood. Especially, when this vitriol is coming from the man who's supposed to have my back, who's supposed to support and encourage—

Ha.

Yeah, that's not the reality on most sports teams.

I'm a commodity, a resource to be used—even if Rome is trying to change things, trying to shift the back office dynamics so we're more of a family than just a group of guys spending nine months together doing the same thing.

Frankly, it's not working all that well.

Oh, we've been winning.

And we have a small subset of like-minded guys.

But we still have Coach. Still have Pat and his idiot crew. Still have—

"Are you even fucking listening to me?" Coach screams, throwing his pen and nearly hitting me with it.

Luckily, I dodge, manage to not lose my fucking eye. "I'm listening," I say quietly, after he's finished his screaming fit. "I've got it. And I'll fix it."

"See that you fucking do," he snaps, slamming down the tablet he's been using to show me replays of my indiscretions on the ice (as though I didn't fucking know them already, as though they weren't already on repeat in my mind). "Dismissed."

Cool. Cool. So. *Much*. Fun.

I inhale. Exhale.

Shove down my anger.

Then push up to my feet and move out into the hall, nearly running into Pat.

Of course he's fucking here.

Wearing his trademark smirk.

Unfortunately for me, the fucker played great tonight—he seems to do better the worse I play, like he's loving every bit of my torment, like he senses the shit tearing me up inside even though no one aside from my doctor and I know what's going on.

It doesn't impact the team.

It's none of their business.

Except…it *is* impacting the team, isn't it?

A throb begins in my temple—or maybe it's always there and it just ramps up being in the presence of this asshole.

"Jackson," he begins, his condescending tone telling me he heard every fucking word of Coach's verbal reaming even before he finishes the statement. He reaches into his pocket and pulls out a handful of disgusting-looking tissues. "Do you need to go cry about it?"

Jesus fucking Christ.

I can't with this asshole.

I start to push by him, but he puts up his hand, as though to stop me.

"Touch me, fuck face," I growl, "and I'll fucking break it off. I don't care how many goals you've scored this season."

His brows shoot up. "Tsk. Tsk. So touchy."

Luckily, before he can say anything else—or I make good on

my threat and break it the fuck off—Coach bellows, "Franklin, get your ass in here!"

Pat smirks and salutes me, disappearing into Coach's office. Though, he doesn't close the door all the way, and I hear Coach take on a decidedly friendly tone as he says, "Nice going out there, Franklin. I really liked your intensity and…"

I don't bother to hang around and listen to the two assholes jerk each other off, just haul my ass to the showers, thankful that most of the guys are gone—having either moved on to be seen by the training stuff or already heading home.

Unfortunately, most isn't *all*.

And when I come out of the showers, it's to find King and Rome sitting on either side of my locker.

Jesus Christ. I don't have the time or patience for this shit.

I grind my teeth together—something that seems to be my M.O. of late—and try to cheer myself up by thinking my dentist will be happy with the extra work. Then I move over to them, trying to make short work of getting dressed so I don't have to deal with this shit.

Shit, of course, being my friends concerned about me.

It's just…

I was fine.

Totally fine.

And then…I wasn't.

"What the fuck's going on with you?" King asks with all the directness of an older brother with a gaggle of younger siblings. My oldest bro, Carter, has that too—the innate candor and limited patience for bullshit. The difference is that King and all of his brothers play hockey, so he knows there's something affecting my game and it's not the normal ebb and flow of a season—something I could slip by my siblings without them really knowing.

They love me, love what I do…they don't know the sport like King does.

Like *Rome* does.

Who's fixing me in place with an expression I don't fucking like. It tells me he's seeing far too much. *Again*. And it tells me that he's running out of patience for my avoidance.

"Look," I hedge, "I know I've had a couple of rough games, but I'm tired."

King's mouth kicks up and Rome's expression doesn't change—their ways of telling me that they don't buy that bullshit excuse at all.

"It's true," I say. "My family was here and they're a lot, even when they're trying to be unobtrusive. So, I'm out of my normal routine and haven't been able to catch up on my sleep. But they're home now and I've got nothing but video games, gym time, and bed rot for the next two days. I'll be back to myself by next game."

King's mouth has flattened out during that verbal vomit.

Rome's still looks exactly the same.

Not buying it. At all.

But if I've learned anything from being the youngest in my big ass family, it's that to show weakness now is to forfeit all right to privacy and self-actualization.

They're already up in my shit.

If these two know something is *really* going on, they'll be so entrenched in my life that I won't be take a piss by myself.

So…I need to distract these assholes.

Who are my friends.

Who I care about.

Who are…*fine*.

All right.

Who are *not* assholes.

They're family, but still, I need to distract them so I can fuck off out of here, go home, and get my shit together.

Which is why I drop my towel—knowing they'll look away, that they'll give me a second to think—and start getting dressed. I take a breath, think fast, and ask, "What have you two got going on our days off?"

"Gym," Rome says. "But mostly recovery and Chrissy's got a climb she wants to try, so I'm on kitten duty," he adds. "Unless you want to come over and scoop those litter boxes?"

"No thanks," I mutter. "Though I *can* employ my feather toy skills."

King snorts.

I yank down my sweatshirt as I turn to him and continue with Operation Distraction. "What are you and Rory up to?"

"Recovery too," he says. "Just not at home."

I lift my brows.

"I'm taking her to the coast for the day," he says, softening in a way I've only ever seen him do with the woman he loves. "She's never been down to Carmel. Can you believe that? We'll go, soak up the beach for a few hours and eat some good food, and then I'm going to fuck her while listening to the ocean from our hotel room."

My mouth twitches. "King Bang strikes again?"

He socks me, albeit not that hard. Mostly because Kingston Bang has been known around the league as King Bang for as long as I can remember—the infamous womanizer who's finally succumbed to love.

He's heard the nickname far too often to truly be bothered by it.

"Then it'll be like that one"—he nods to Rome—"gym, fuel up, recover, and get ready to win the next game."

"What hotel are you taking her to?" I ask.

He tells us and then Rome asks about restaurants, and pretty soon the distraction of their women means that I'm able to finish getting dressed without an inquisition, able to get in my car, drive home, and walk into my quiet house without further delay.

I grab my post-game snack, and head for the den.

I just want to kill some fucking monsters, want to focus on anything except the game, on anything but the secrets that have been tearing me up, on anything except the news I got this morning. The final news—no more chances, no more changes, no more tests to be run.

That's that.

Now I just…need to deal with it.

Put it behind me.

Buck up and move on.

Which would be a little easier if it was something I didn't realize I wanted until too late.

I pick up the controller, start logging in to my game.

Then realize it's fucking late, we have a playoff game that can end our season in three days, and…

I'm using my toys to soothe me.

Like a child.

"Jesus, man," I mutter, dropping the controller and pushing up from the couch. I just need to cut the crap, go the fuck to sleep, and wake up with a better mindset.

Easy. Done.

Sure it is.

But it's something for me to focus on as I head upstairs, eat my snack, and then climb into bed.

Something for me to cling to as my dreams are filled with…

Nightmares.

CHAPTER SIX

Ats

I CLOSE the file and lean back in my desk chair, staring at my computer screen and trying to make the facts fit.

Lex and I spent almost five years trying to close down an organized crime ring that centered around the small coastal town of Stoneybrook on the other side of the country.

We finally cracked it when we managed to nail the ringleader —Frankie's dad.

Yeah, it's complicated and made shit seriously heavy for Lex when he was falling in love with her, but the bosses of the Lyon crime ring were eventually taken down, Frankie was cleared, and her and Lex could ride off with their happily ever after into the sunset.

But that doesn't mean all parties who were working for the Lyons just turned over a new leaf and got on the straight and narrow. The lifelong criminals we weren't able to take down didn't start volunteering for senior charities or to paint over graffiti on the side of buildings or to clean up dog poop assholes leave on the street.

They're still out there.

Still doing illegal shit.

Still hurting people.

And one of them killed Tommy.

I rub the throb in my temple and sigh.

I just don't know which one.

Same as I can't be *absolutely* certain that a group of those Lyon criminals—the mid- to high-level bastards who managed to slip out from beneath our net—are in the Bay Area.

I just...*feel* it.

The pieces seem to line up. My gut tells me I'm right.

But then again, my gut led to Tommy getting killed, so what the fuck do I know?

I exhale again, rub more determinedly at the throb.

I'll find him. I know I will.

I just need to keep working, keep pulling the pieces together, keep—

There's a knock at the door and I look up, see my new boss, Sandra, leaning back against the door frame. "Pack it in."

I frown. "What?"

"It's seven-thirty," she says. "You've been here since six"—I open my mouth to play dumb, but she talks over me—"cameras, Ats, plus you know that Connie keeps track of everyone's hours, so don't try to bullshit me."

Suitably chastised, I close my mouth.

Connie is the office mom—and just like most good moms in the world, she has her fingers on the pulses of all of the agents in her department.

Which means there's no way I can lie my way through this.

"I know I'm close," I mutter.

"Says every agent, all the fucking time," Sandra quips then tilts her head to the hall. "Pack it up, pack it out. We're going to the bar."

"No, I'll—"

"Grab your shit and come out with us," she interrupts, absolutely no room for argument in her tone.

Fucking hell.

I look longingly at my computer.

"Don't even think about it." Another tilt of her head to the hall. "Come on. I'll even buy you a beer."

Knowing I've lost, I give in with a sigh, log off, and grab my jacket and purse.

And then…

I follow her.

————

SCOWLING, I sit on my stool, nursing my beer at a local hotspot called Bobby's.

It's all sticky old wood and blond oak tables. A bar that's seen some things—

At least in *this* room.

The front of Bobby's almost made me turn around and walk right the fuck out—Sandra's interference and Connie's wrath or not.

But, sensing my impending tactical retreat, Sandra had slipped her arm through mine and drew me through the dance music and flashing lights, through the throng of young bodies rubbing all over each other, down the hall, and into—

A much better space—in my opinion, anyway.

The old-timers hanging in their usual spots, a group of women who look like they've been friends for years cackling around a table in the corner, bartenders who know their patrons' names, and us—a group of new colleagues sitting awkwardly at a high top table.

Luckily, the Eagles game is on and providing distraction.

Mostly because it's a battle as the match winds down in the third period, the Eagles down a goal and looking to tie it up.

Cam is looking to tie it up. I can see his focus when the camera pans to him on the bench, can see how hard he's working when he's on the ice. And he's flying around, skating faster than should be possible, slamming his body into guys on the other team, getting knocked down in front of the net, blocking shots—

Doing all the things I've seen him do in the many games I've watched.

But…

It doesn't seem to be enough.

None of what he or the other guys on the Eagles do seems to be enough.

Not with under two minutes left between them and the end of the season.

"Damn," I hear and blink, refocusing on the game, realizing the commercial break is over and the play's started up again. The specks—one of which is Cam—speed around on the ice.

But, I realize, not in the direction we want.

They're zipping toward the Eagles' net, and I spot Cam trying to catch up with a fast fucker from the other team. He's closing the distance—

"Come on," I whisper.

Five feet behind.

I clench my beer.

Two feet, almost close enough to reach the puck, but he's also almost out of room. Their goalie is right there and there's a guy from the other team who's caught up too and—

"Shit," I whisper, realizing that Cam's already seen what I've only just clocked.

He dives to disrupt the pass…

Too late.

The puck flies across the front of the net.

Lands right on the other guy's stick.

And—

I lean forward.

Then close my eyes, shoulders sinking as everyone watching the game groans.

When I open them again, it's to see the guys from the Grizzlies hugging each other and slamming into the boards, to see Cam—his front covered in snow, his expression slicing my insides to ribbons—push up to his skates and head to the bench.

His Coach leans in and I can't hear him obviously, but I can see his face, can see that it's not encouragement.

And those claws rake across my insides again.

Cam. Well…he doesn't deserve that.

And maybe that's why, as I watch the Eagles go out with renewed energy, as they battle all the way down until the final buzzer goes, I decide to do what I do next.

Regardless of how dumb.

————

"THIS IS FUCKING STUPID," I mutter an hour later as I jab at the keypad that will open the garage door, holding the six-pack of beer bottles under one arm, the paper bag under the other.

My purse swings forward and whacks me in the face as I squint and try to see the numbers, trying to remember the code Martha put in.

Knowing without a doubt that I'm overstepping.

And breaking and entering.

But is it really breaking and entering if I know the code to get in?

Pushing that prevarication aside, I sigh in relief as the keypad flashes green and the heavy metal garage door begins rumbling open. Then I'm walking across the shadowed space, twisting the knob and giving another relieved sigh when it twists, when I can pull it open, when there's no alarm for me to contend with inside.

I need to have a talk with Cam about safety.

But later.

I hit the button to send the garage door sliding closed then walk down the hall.

Into the kitchen.

And I settle in to wait.

CHAPTER SEVEN

Cam

WE LOST.

Lost the game.

Lost the fucking season.

Lost my fucking job likely.

Groaning softly, I slip out of the quiet locker room. The press has grilled us all—I've heard no little amount of *"You were first in the league and now you're out in the first round, what happened?"*

We've all given our excuses, know that the broadcasters and bloggers will be taking their pound of flesh in the days to come.

We've congratulated the other team during the handshake at center ice, saluted our fans.

We've listened to Coach rant.

And we've listened to Rome do his best to be a good captain, to put a good spin on it.

But…

None of it—the yelling, the *keep-your-heads-ups*, the questions—make us, or at least *me*, feel better.

Not good enough.

Not *enough* in general.

I walk down the hall, head straight for my car, and get the fuck out of there.

No doubt, most of the guys are going to find someone to fuck their frustrations out on, and most of *them* are going to do it while getting rip-roaring drunk.

I'm going home to get drunk and slaughter my way through an orc village.

It's better than empty sex—better than the feelings that empty sex leaves me with—*and* I won't have to interact with anyone aside from my online friends.

No family, who've blown up my phone with calls and texts and voicemails.

No teammates, who're feeling this as much as I am—most of them, anyway.

No assistant coaches or training staff or captains, trying to make us feel better after Coach screamed down the room.

Just…mindless activity until I pull my head together.

The roads are quiet, the post-game traffic having cleared out in the time that it took to take care of all my shit, so my drive home is smooth and relatively quick.

I hit the button to open the garage, pull in, and head inside, hanging up my bag and taking off my shoes in the mud room. I want a post-game snack, but it sure as shit isn't going to be my normal healthy version. I'm thinking something my mom stashed in my freezer and a family sized bag of tortilla chips to cover both sweet and salty, all washed down with enough beer that I sleep for a solid ten hours.

Good plan. Go. *Break.*

I'm so focused on that plan that I miss the light on in the kitchen.

But I sure as shit don't miss the woman sitting at the island.

Thank God I hung my shit up, otherwise it would have ended up on the floor.

"A-Athena?" I stammer.

She'd started swiveling in my direction, but my use of her full name has her glaring at me.

"Ats," I correct quickly. "What"—the *fuck*—"are you doing here?"

There's a flurry of emotions across her pretty brown eyes before she turns fully to face me. "It was a rough game, huh?"

I still, a flurry of emotions now running through *me*. "That's the job," I say, moving to the fridge, intent on that beer—

"Uh-hum."

I turn and see her holding up a beer—and more than that, a bottle of my favorite local IPA—and I hesitate, heart pounding, hope slicing all through my insides, tangling with confusion, with not knowing what the hell is going on or how to handle the woman I'm obsessed with being in my house, coming here like this.

She wiggles the bottle again, and I snap into motion, moving over and taking it, trying not to stare.

But I know I do anyway, searching for more freckles on the bridge of her nose, for the softer brown highlights in her curls that signify her spending time in the sun. I inhale, get that whiff of pure Athena—jasmine and vanilla and *woman.*

Thankfully, she moves, snapping me out of my reverie, and I focus on the bag.

On what she's pulling *out* of the bag.

"It's not one of your mom's confectioneries," she says, flattening the brown paper and setting it on top, "and I'll admit that I had half of it for breakfast." I must make a sound because her eyes dart to mine and she hurries to add, "I cut it in half with a knife because it's so big. I didn't gnaw it off like a hungry dog or something."

My shock fades, replaced by amusement. "You mean like you do with Mom's cinnamon rolls?"

The pink on her cheeks surprises me. It's fucking adorable and far softer than any side of Ats that I normally see. This whole moment is—the showing up after the game, the beer, the treat she knows I'll love...*all* of it is different than anything I've ever seen from her.

"Your mother's cinnamon rolls must be laced with crack because I'm totally addicted." She grins. "But Molly's bakery is a close second." She pushes the treat toward me. "It's an apple cinnamon turnover."

I push it back. "I don't want to eat your food, Ats."

"Well," she says, her tone growing the tiniest bit sharp, "I don't know how to do this—"

"Do what?"

Her lips press flat.

I move a little closer. "Do what, cupcake?"

Her head shoots up, and I could kick myself as I see the icy shields practically snap back into place.

"Be nice?" I add quickly before she can bolt. "Or be the first line of defense so I don't have a mental breakdown?" I force a smile. "Don't worry. This shit sucks, but I'll be over it in a couple of days."

She narrows her eyes at me. "First," she grits out. "I can be nice."

I snort.

Her glare intensifies. "And I know you're not going to have a mental breakdown," she snaps. "But it's like you said. This sucks and it's nice to not be alone sometimes. If you don't want me here—" She starts to push up out of the chair.

My hand shoots out before I even process it moving, gripping her wrist, halting her retreat.

"I'm sorry, cupcake," I say quietly. "I'm..." I sigh. "Well, I'm in a shit mood. I shouldn't pick at you."

Her gaze flicks from my fingers on her arm up to mine. "I'd be in a shit mood too." She presses her lips together then releases them softly and adds, "Especially when someone's invaded your house."

My mouth kicks up. "You say that as though I'm not used to being invaded."

"That's true," she agrees quietly, slipping her wrist free. I can feel the imprint of her skin on my fingertips. "But still annoying."

"Ats—"

"So, what were you planning on doing?" she asks quickly. "Heading up to bed?" The pink in her cheeks flares.

I study it, hope filling my insides nearly to bursting.

Is this…?

Does her being here mean…?

"I should go," she blurts. "Let you rest."

"I can never fall asleep after games," I say before she can push up to her feet again.

Before she can leave.

"Adrenaline rush," she says, and it's not a question. "I feel that."

I bet she does.

Especially since she's spent the last decade navigating a career that's far more dangerous and adrenaline-inducing than mine.

"So, what do you do to wind down then?" she asks a moment later.

I shrug, feeling my own cheeks going pink. "Play video games, drink a beer—though tonight I'll have more than one—" I pause, realizing belatedly how that sounds.

She raises her hands, palms out. "Hey. No judgment here. I absolutely know the medicinal purposes of tying one on."

"Yeah," I mutter, not sure I believe that.

She nudges the turnover my direction. Plunks another beer in front of me. "So we eat. We drink." Then she winks. "And then… we video game."

———

"NO!" she shouts. "No. No. *No!* Ugh." She drops the controller to the couch and flops onto the cushions.

Normally, losing a raid would be frustrating, but…

Fuck, she's beautiful.

Fuck, I'm drunk.

Fuck, I want to kiss her, to hold her, to tell her how I feel.

How I've *felt* for so long.

But…

Her feelings for Lex.

And Christ, she's just trying to do something nice for me.

She doesn't need my shit.

Even *if* she's beautiful in the pale light of the den, her curls a riot around her face, her brows furrowed in concentration as she picks up her controller and begins again.

I love her.

I want her.

I—

Fuck, I'm pathetic.

I exhale and scrub a hand over my face, something that draws her attention.

She pauses the game, glances over at me. "You ready for bed yet?"

Only if you come with me.

Jesus, Cam.

"I'm fine," I say, shoving that thought out of my head and picking up my beer, taking a long sip. It's number…well, *number* enough that the edges of my focus are blurred, that these thoughts—dreams, fantasies—about Athena are coming free and loose. "Let's finish this first," I say. "You're finally getting the hang of it."

"*Finally*, huh?" she teases.

And the words are torn from me without conscious approval.

"You're beautiful, you know that right?"

Athena goes completely still.

For long enough that I know I've totally gone and FUBARed this night.

"I just—"

There's a screech on the screen, a dragon appearing out of nowhere, my fictional universe sweeping in to save the day when I clearly can't.

"Oh shit," she says. "What do I do?"

"Right trigger and hit X like a motherfucker," I order as I grab my controller and hurry over to where she's getting decimated, pulling out my weapons, going ham on the creature, if only because it gives me something to do that isn't being an idiot.

I kill it, walking my fictional druid back a good distance away, and then give her some further instructions, talking her through the entrance of the dungeon we're trying to beat.

And I do it while finishing off my beer.

And then another.

I keep drinking as we *finally* survive the raid.

And as my lids grow heavy and we head back to town to deposit our gold.

And as she asks me questions and puts a couple of items up for sale at the game's auction house.

I keep drinking until all the beer bottles are empty and I'm drunk enough that I have to close my eyes, just for a second.

And I know I drank far too much when I wake up in the morning with a splitting headache, a clean den, a blanket spread out over me, and—

No sign that Athena had been there at all.

Except for the paper bag from Molly's sitting on the countertop.

And the sense that my hangover is from being drunk on Athena's presence…

Not the beers.

CHAPTER EIGHT

I SIGH and inhale the cool mountain air.

It's warm down in the Bay—not blistering like mid-August will get, just definitely edging into summer. But up in the Sierras, only a couple of hours away, it's the perfect mix of cool and balmy.

I loved living in Stoneybrook, loved being *right* next to the Atlantic.

The sand, the surf, the whitecaps in the distance…all beautiful.

But there's something unreal about these mountains. Maybe it's the granite slabs protruding up to the sky. Maybe it's the conifers huddled in tight clumps together all the way up to the tree line, the pockets of snow that cling to the clefts and valleys, despite the incoming summer season. Or maybe it's the rivers that parallel the highway on the way up, parts both fast and slowly bubbling, or filled with rapids and smoothly flowing, dotted with huge boulders and fallen trees and bridges that cross the river, giving access to quaint cabins and winter houses.

It's…Stoneybrook in the mountains.

It's…so far away from the concrete and buildings where I grew up. Only a few hours away but with little to no greenspace. No mountains or fresh air or freedom.

I inhale and exhale again, know that I need to get into my car and drive back home.

The lead we were investigating was a bust, and everyone's headed down the mountain to enjoy the long weekend.

I need to do the same, especially with the dark clouds in the distance coming in.

But…

I take one more deep breath, stare out at the blue waters of Lake Tahoe, and hold tight to this quiet moment. Then I release a long exhale, get in my car, and start driving home.

I'm just ascending the mountains that lead out of the valley when my cell rings.

"Lex," I say, answering the call with a jab at the screen that will send it blaring through my car's speakers. "Hey."

"You're up in Tahoe right?" he asks without preamble.

I frown as I navigate a hairpin turn. "Yeah. Why? Did you find something with the case?"

"No."

Disappointment weaves through me, but I tamp that down. "So, what's up?"

"It's Cam."

That disappointment is displaced with worry and I have to pause before I speak so my voice is steady. "What's wrong with Cam?"

Lex sighs. "He's up there, just outside the basin, but incommunicado. I'm sure he's fine and just licking his wounds, especially after his asshole coach put him on blast on social media."

I wince.

Even though I don't follow sports blogging, the post with the video of the Eagles head coach, Peter Auclair, lambasting his players—but most especially Cam—has gone viral enough that even I've seen it.

And add his attitude with Cam on the bench in the playoffs.

And the pain in Cam's eyes at the end of the season, after losing that game.

And—

"Asshole," I mutter.

"Yup," Lex agrees and I can picture him leaning back in his chair, balancing it on its two rear legs. "Cam's a tough kid, has to be considering how far he's gotten, so I'm sure he's fine. But Martha's worried and frankly, it's not like him to not get in touch."

I frown as I pull into a turnout and park so I can properly focus on the conversation. "How long has it been since she's talked to him?"

"A few days. He was texting back until yesterday, but then stopped replying to everyone—including me."

My frown deepens.

Definitely nothing like the youngest Jackson.

"I can check in on him," I say before he can ask. "You'll send the address?"

My phone vibrates in my pocket.

"Already did."

Despite the concern writhing through my insides, I can't help but smile.

Of course he has.

"Let me plug this into my map," I say, pulling out my phone and pasting the address into the app, hitting the button to pull up the routes. "I'll update you when I make contact with him."

Where he's staying is barely ten minutes down the road.

Good.

"*After* you've read him the riot act for worrying Martha." His voice hardens. "She's barely slept the last few days and was actually looking up flights when I came over."

I narrow my eyes.

Making his lovely, sweet mother lose sleep. Yeah, that's not okay.

Riot act first.

Texting Lex second.

"Damn fucking right I will," I say and hang up.

THEN PULL BACK onto the road.

And as I drive, I already start planning the lecture I'll be giving Cam Jackson.

———

HIS CAR IS PARKED in front of the isolated cabin, taking up most of the space, but I manage to squeeze my little sedan onto the other side of the narrow bridge that spans the rapidly flowing river.

No smooth streams here.

It's all white, frothy water splitting over rocks and tree limbs as it flies rapidly downstream, the runoff from the snow melt intensely fast.

But I make it over the bridge that looks like it won't support a tricycle, cram my car next to Cam's, and shut off the engine.

A gust of wind tugs at my hair as I pop open my door and get out, sending a strand forward, a curl jabbing at my eye. "Ugh," I grunt, wrestling it away as I snag my purse and lock up. The likelihood of anyone stealing it or my car are slim.

But slim isn't zero, so one can't be too careful.

And…

That's enough delaying, I know, as I move up to the cabin's front door.

You're beautiful.

The reason I didn't go back to check on him.

I was feeling too much. Thinking about him too much.

And now….adding guilt to that mix.

I saw the video, knew he was upset, and I hadn't bothered to circle back—

No.

I'd *avoided* it.

Even though the Jacksons had treated me like…

Family.

And just because I was uncomfortable and weak and scared, I'd—

"Enough," I whisper, shoving the past down with ruthless authority.

The problem is that Cam had said those words once before.

In the middle of a different night, as though it was only the two of us awake in the entire universe.

That was…uncomfortable.

It had made me run, made me distance myself.

Until Lex all but smacked me around—or bribed me with cinnamon rolls—to get me to attend another Jackson event.

Cam wasn't there.

He'd made it to the NHL.

So, he wasn't there for a lot of events over the years.

And…I guess I'd forgotten.

Or buried my response to his words, to the way his intense stare had pinned me in place, as though he'd seen me—*all* of me.

But it all came rushing back two weeks ago.

And all those feelings were so much stronger because…

Cam's not just the youngest Jackson any longer.

Sitting next to him on the couch, smelling the spicy scent of him, seeing the stubble on his cheeks, critically aware of the strength of him as he sat so close, as he patiently taught me how to play a video game had been so much more.

It began because I was worried about him.

It ended with me tucking a blanket around his sleeping form…but wanting to crawl onto the couch next to him.

I didn't, of course.

Instead, I got the hell out of his house before I said or did something stupid.

And I worked with more of that ruthless authority.

And now…I'm here.

Sighing, I clomp up the three stairs leading to the narrow porch—not bothering to be quiet—and reach forward to jab at the doorbell.

I hear it go off inside, listen for footsteps.

And wait.

"Jesus," I grumble, jabbing at the button again, impatiently waiting, and after a third ring goes unanswered, I mutter a curse and try the handle.

The metal knob turns under my palm.

"Idiot," I mutter, knowing I *really* need to talk to him about safety, before I push inside, closing the door behind me.

The house is dark and quiet, and my nape prickles as I move into the hall, gaze scanning the space, half-expecting to find him parked in front of the TV with his headphones on, unable to hear me as he games with his online friends.

But the TV is off and the entire space is lifeless.

My fingers itch with the urge to reach for my gun, carefully tucked into my holster, but I resist the impulse and move down the narrow hall to the back of the cabin.

One door is a linen closet.

Another is a bathroom.

One more an empty bedroom—

Or not *so* empty because Cam is sprawled out on the bed.

My throat threatens to close up, heat blazing through me when I realize that he's—

Buck ass naked.

Sweet baby Jesus.

He shifts and I quickly avert my gaze, but not before seeing—

Ho, mama.

No.

Not *ho, mama.*

I feel nothing but concern, nothing but sisterly worry and an appreciation for a gorgeous ass.

That's it. It's just a butt.

Nothing more. Nothing at all—

"Athena."

For a second, I freeze, thinking he's awake, that he's spotted me standing in the open doorway, staring at his ass.

But then I realize he's not—mostly because of what he does next.

He rolls to his back, hand drifting south, wrapping around his cock, and—

"Oh God. *Athena*."

CHAPTER NINE

Cam

I'M HAVING A BLISSFULLY great dream—Athena lying next to me in bed, her hands drifting over all my body, stroking toward my cock, gripping, pumping, and—

A shock of cold shoots through me.

For a second, I think I'm still in my dream, think I'm imagining her with cold hands as she jerks me off.

Then I realize it's not *just* cold.

But…*wet.*

"What the fuck?"

Sleep is gone in an instant and I swipe a hand over my face, sending droplets scattering, squinting and trying to figure out what the fuck is going on. My head is swimming and if I'm not still drunk, I'm definitely buzzed.

"Clean up."

I jerk at the sharp words, nearly jab out my eye as I whip my head around to see Ats standing in the doorway.

"Wake up," she snaps, gaze locked onto mine. "*Clean* up. And get fucking dressed." She spins on her heel, heading for the hall before stopping and glaring at me over her shoulder. "And call your fucking *mother*."

Then she's gone, stomping down the hall.

I'm frozen for probably far too long, half-convinced that I'm still dreaming, but then I become aware of the water droplets.

They're sliding down my chest.

And they're fucking *cold*.

And I'm fucking *naked*.

What the—

There's clattering from the kitchen, so I snap to attention, grabbing the towel and scrubbing it over my face, my hair and my fucking naked body.

I exhale, toss it to the side, stumble over to my duffle shoved in the corner of the room, and yank out some clothes. It takes me just a couple of minutes to get dressed, and the entire time the clanging doesn't stop.

Christ, will I even have a kitchen to return to by the time I get out there?

I hustle down the hall, and I'd be lying if I said my head wasn't spinning, the walls weren't moving.

Maybe beer *and* whisky was a bad idea.

But fuck it.

The off-season is here. The Grizzlies are advancing to the finals and I'm…

Crash.

"Shit," I mutter, turning the corner and heading into the kitchen.

Athena has a pot on the stove, and the fridge door is open, her shapely ass on full display as she pulls open one of the plastic drawers and then slams it closed. "What the fuck is this shit?" she snaps, stomping across the space and throwing open a cabinet before glancing over her shoulder and glaring at me. "Do you *even* have any food fit for human consumption?"

"It's just salad, Ats," I say, tamping down on my dick's reaction to her lush ass. "And protein bars and—"

"Rice and chicken and fucking broccoli," she snaps. "Where's the chocolate? Where's the chips? Where's the junk food you can gorge on?"

"I feel like shit after eating that crap," I mutter.

A huffed-out laugh. "And you don't feel like shit half-drunk after"—she yanks open the top of the freestanding trash can—"downing an entire bottle of whisky and case of beer?"

She has a point.

But I can't bring myself to agree with her.

Because I feel like shit right about now—and that's *with* the buzz still clinging to my brain.

"And to do that all *without* any junk food?" she snaps, throwing up her hands and stomping to the door.

"Where are you going?" I ask when she flings it open so hard it slams into the wall.

A fierce glare over her shoulder before she stomps down the stairs and over to her car, wrenching open that door with a sickening screech. It's starting to rain, the sky clouded over, the drops turning the dirt in front of my cabin into a Pollock-like smattering of dark brown and light.

"Christ," I mutter, scrubbing a hand over my face.

I hear her slam the driver's side door then watch as she storms back over, a tote bag in hand. She shoves by me and moves into the kitchen, slamming it down onto the old wooden table.

"What are you doing?" I ask as she reaches inside the canvas bag.

"Offering up my Car Snacks to a dumbass hockey player," she mutters. "Close the door." A snapped-out order. "It's getting fucking cold out there."

Right.

The wind's blowing, those drops falling harder.

A storm's coming in.

I frown, study the sky, the river, then open my mouth to tell her that it looks bad and she should go—

"And fucking lock it this time," she snaps, distracting me. "Since you're going to stop being an idiot and remember that doors have locks and bad guys are everywhere and you're not usually a goddamned idiot when it comes to your personal safety!"

Confusion is shoved out by annoyance. "Look, Ats," I grind out. "I don't know why you're here, but I didn't ask for a Jackson invasion."

"You've been out of contact for several days. Haven't returned calls or texts—" She fixes me in place with another fierce glare. "And your mom is worried."

That, like nothing else, is what tamps down my frustration.

My mom's worried?

"Fuck," I mutter, any vestiges of my drunkenness disappearing like so much smoke.

"Yeah," she says, slamming down a bowl and dumping ingredients inside. "*Exactly.*" A nod to my cell, sitting haphazardly on the coffee table where I must have left it before I put it on Do Not Disturb and passed out.

And also why I hadn't heard it ring—

I unlock it, glance at the screen, see that the battery is low, and…

That there are twenty calls and near-on one hundred messages.

Damn.

They weren't all directed at me—the bulk were from our family's group chat. Pictures of the kids, comments on how cute they are, an event at Frankie's shop with all of Stoneybrook seeming to show up. Misty had knitted a new blanket for Chloe and they were planning a summer trip and wanted opinions on where to go.

But a handful *were* sent only to me.

Damn.

I scroll through them, delete the voicemails without listening to them—the transcripts my phone shows me are enough.

They're worried.

But most especially my mom.

I hit the button for her contact listing, lift the phone to my ear when the call connects and begins ringing.

And doesn't finish.

Because she picks up almost immediately.

Double damn.

"Cam, honey," she says quickly. "Are you okay?"

Not good enough. Not ever enough.

The thoughts cut deeply, but there will be plenty of time for guilt later. "I'm fine, Mom. Sorry I worried you. I was playing with my friends, had a bit too much to drink, and was sleeping it off."

There's a long moment of silence.

"It's summer, remember?" I find myself filling in the quiet, not wanting to hear the disappointment that I know is sure to follow. "We worked our asses off, and I just…needed a break. Don't worry," I add with a laugh. "I'm not twenty-one anymore. The hangover isn't worth it. Neither are the extra hours I'll have to do in the gym to make up for the crap I've been eating the last few days."

"Oh, honey," she says, and her next words tell me that I've curbed her worry and focused her on the right thing.

My stomach.

Instead of my brain and heart—both of which are hurting.

Have been hurting.

But I don't want to think about that.

Thankfully, she picks up on the thread and runs with it. "I know that you've got to hit your micros—or whatever that stuff is called—but it's the off-season now. You deserve to take that break."

"Well, I definitely had one," I remind her, keeping my tone deliberately light. "And it's macros, by the way."

"Pish," she says. "Micros. Macros. Same difference. Now,

when will you be back in the Bay? I'm going to send you some food."

I smile, despite the throb in my head, despite my heart hurting because of…

"Next week. But as tempting as it is for you to overnight some of your lasagna," I tell her, "I think I'd better find my way back to my food plan."

Athena snorts, but I ignore her and spend the next couple of minutes talking my mom down from the food mailing edge.

I love her.

She's amazing.

But I really just need to be off the phone with her.

"Fine," she eventually relents, "but since we've decided we're taking our vacation on your coast—"

"I told you I'd visit in a few weeks so you don't have—"

She ignores me. "—I'll make sure you eat well then."

"Mom—"

"Oh," she says, distraction creeping into her tone. "Your dad's home and we're meeting the McCaulys for dinner. I'll talk to you soon, honey, okay?"

"I—"

"Love you, baby boy. Bye!"

I barely get my goodbye out before she's clicking off.

The whirlwind is gone, and I exhale.

"You're not really going to give up Car Snacks for salad, are you?"

CHAPTER TEN

Ats

HE GLANCES UP, his hazel eyes filled with confusion for a
moment.

Then it clears and his mouth kicks up.

Gorgeous.

He shakes his head. "I'd *never* give up Car Snacks." A beat.
"What exactly are Car Snacks?"

I roll my eyes, hate that my anger is ebbing.

I've made the stop when I should be well on my way home—
yes, it wasn't really all that far off my planned route, but it *was* a
stop, and he was drunk and in an unlocked house and fucking
naked.

I grind my teeth together.

Naked is the smallest problem in this scenario.

Okay, well not the *smallest*—

Fuck, Ats. Just stop.

He gets up, but instead of reaching toward the pile of Car
Snacks like I expect, he pushes off the couch and heads into the
kitchen.

"What are you doing?" I ask.

"I wasn't kidding with my mom. I drank my calories these last few days. My body needs green things and some protein."

I wrinkle my nose because that sounds awful.

"And *then* I need my empty calories."

Okay so that's a *little* better.

I rip open a candy bar and make my way back into the kitchen.

"Not pissed any longer?" he teases.

"You're alive and talked to your mom," I say. "You text the family group chat and stay sober enough to not go incommunicado again *and* lock your fucking door, and you'll be clear in my books."

He glances at me then pulls his phone from his pocket and taps at the screen. "Done on the text. Noted on the lock. And you saw my fridge and cabinets—I've emptied the bulk of my alcohol stash."

I *have* seen the state of his fridge—chicken and broccoli, yogurt and fancy protein shakes.

Fucking lame.

But also very Cam. And very much *not* like a man who's going to drink himself into an early grave.

He starts pulling ingredients out and heads to the counter to prep. "It's getting dark out there and the rain's falling harder."

I pause and realize the sound I'm hearing is raindrops hitting the roof.

"You should leave soon, or you'll need to stay. The roads will be unsafe."

I have complete confidence in my ability to navigate bad roads—I've taken the driving classes, have the certifications, have the experience driving through many a winding, dark road.

But he wants me to leave.

And that prickles enough of my senses that I don't go out the door, get in my car, and start heading back down the mountains.

Instead, I grab my pile of snacks, sit at the table, and watch as he prepares something disgustingly healthy.

He doesn't break the silence, though, and I find myself sitting here and watching him, trying to figure out what the hell feels so wrong about this whole situation…

And what feels so right.

And why I want to get up and walk over to him, to pinch that ass and see if it's as firm as it appeared when he was naked.

Because it looked like I could bounce a fucking dime off it, or take a bite—

I nearly choke on my candy bar.

Enough.

This is Cam Jackson.

Baby Jackson.

I cannot be thinking of his ass or his big dick or—

Thunk.

I jump as he sets a plate in front of me then one in front of the chair across from me and folds his big body into it.

"Eat," he orders quietly, passing me a napkin and fork. "And don't bitch about the green stuff. It's good for you."

"It may be good for me," I mutter, but I pick up the fork and start eating, finding myself pleasantly surprised by the taste—it's not have bad, but, "it's still green."

Mirth in his golden-green eyes. "Yeah, baby. It's still green."

My lungs freeze, and I know I should tell him off for using that endearment, but…

I can't.

It settles somewhere in me, across a deep-seated wound that I didn't know I had.

A man calling me *baby*. A man cooking me dinner. A man looking after me.

I mentally slap myself.

I'm fine. I can take care of myself and—

"Can I have a Snickers?"

I look up, shocked to see his plate is already empty, and roll my eyes before passing over the requested candy bar. "Jackson hollow leg syndrome strikes again?"

A big shoulder lifts and drops. "Not my fault that you pick at your veggies like a toddler."

I purposely stab a piece of broccoli, shove it in my mouth, and chew. "See?" I say around my bite. "I can eat my vegetables."

It just doesn't mean I like them.

A grin. "Yes, I can see that you're enjoying them so much."

"Not my fault you can't cook."

His grin widens. "Rude, Ats."

There's a mix of relief and disappointment when he uses my name instead of *baby*, but I push it aside, finish the green stuff, and then start in on the chicken. "You're not a half-bad cook."

"And you bring good Car Snacks."

I roll my eyes. "Cool it with the cockiness, mister. I'm still pissed I had to come and wake up your drunk ass."

That grin fades, and I kick myself. "I'm sorry."

I set down my fork. "No," I say. "I'm being a bitch. I was worried about you and mad you left the door unlocked and frustrated that you scared your family."

And that you were naked, and I saw—

Enough.

Fucking *enough.*

"I really *am* sorry," he says again. "You shouldn't have had to come here and—"

"I was already in Tahoe," I say quickly. "Lex called and it took no time to pop over, Cam." His expression doesn't change, and I reach over and take his hand. "I mean it. I was pissed when you were here, and I found you sleeping. I just...I was concerned that something really bad happened and—"

I had more words on the tip of my tongue, but the pain that tears through his eyes, ripples across his face has them stoppering up in the back of my throat.

What the fuck?

What the *actual* fuck?

"Is it the video?"

He blinks and the emotions are gone, carefully tucked away. "Coach was an asshole, that's for sure, but that's professional sports, and it's not like it's the first time he's put the team on blast."

"You," I murmur. "He put *you* on blast."

Cam rubs his forehead and sighs. "Yeah, that fucking stings." He bites off half of the candy bar, chews and swallows. "But I'll get over it. Bonus is I have a few months to stew on it before I go back to work."

"So, what's really bothering you then?"

He frowns. "Nothing."

A blatant fucking lie.

"Bullshit."

"Ats," he says on a sigh. "I drank a couple of beers and some whisky, did some raids with my friends. You played that game. You know how addictive and distracting it can be."

His game *is* addictive and distracting, and I've personally experienced how easy it is to lose a few hours to it.

But also…

This has been going on long before the end of the season.

"Bullshit," I say again, more firmly this time.

He opens his mouth, but I slice my hand through the air.

"Cut the crap, Cam." I drop my hands onto the table and lean forward, my gaze locked onto his. "I know it's more than what's going on with the Eagles. You were off before the season was over."

"I'm fine," he lies. "I've *been* fine."

"Nope. Not fucking buying it. Try that shit with someone else."

"Athena—"

"Ats," I correct. "But neither *Athena* nor I believe the bullshit you're trying to spin."

He sighs, opens his mouth.

I wave my hand at him. "If excuses are about to come out of there then I don't want to hear them."

A growl rumbles from his chest and it's fucking hot, same as the anger clinging to the edges of his eyes.

Would he fuck angry?

Would it be as glorious as I think it would be?

And...I shouldn't be thinking that, but I'm only fucking human.

"Ats."

I lift my brows.

"You should go."

I cross my arms. "Not until you tell me the truth."

He tosses up his hands. "There's nothing to tell."

"Again. *Bullshit.*"

Another growl, but this time he drops his own hands on the table and leans toward me, our faces just inches apart. "It's *not* bullshit," he grits out.

"*Liar,*" I say, ignoring my pulse speeding through my veins, the urge to close the distance between us and kiss him.

Yes, I'm losing my mind.

But this is more important.

"I'm not—"

"L.I.A.R," I spell jauntily.

"The roads—" he attempts.

"Are fine." I shake my head at him. "And you're still lying. *Tell* me, Cam. Tell me what the fuck is happening in that brain of yours."

"It's *fine.*"

"Liar, liar, pants on fire," I taunt. "You are so full of shit. I can see it from here. And I'm not fucking leaving until you clue me in, so just shut up, spit it out, and just fucking *tell me.*"

"Ats—"

"Tell me."

"*Athena—*"

"Tell. Me."

I see it then.

The final thread of his temper snapping—and Jesus, it took him long enough. I watch the fury in him expand, and I hear it too, exploding out through his words.

"I can't fucking have kids, okay?"

CHAPTER ELEVEN

Cam

I CAN'T BELIEVE I said that.

I can't believe I said that.

I open my mouth to take it back, to lie, to hedge, to…fucking *something*, anything but acknowledge the expression on her face, the pain in her eyes.

But…I can't.

I just…

Fucking *can't*.

She leans closer and her palm settles against my cheek, and all of a sudden the tension leeches out of the room. I almost sag into my chair but then she rounds the table, shoves her way between me and the old oak surface, and wraps her arms around me.

I don't breathe—or maybe I *can't* breathe as she hugs me tight.

It's right.

Perfect—just like the last time.

Lithe muscles and womanly curves. Jasmine and vanilla in

my nose, along with hints of chocolate and spice from the candy she shared and the dinner I made. Strong arms wrapped around my middle.

Not a gentle, weak-armed hug.

But…*more.*

Athena's warrior strength and gentle heart on full display as she steps back and drops her hand on my shoulder, pushes me down into my chair. She sits down in the chair next to mine and orders, "Tell me."

And…for the first time since I got the news, I crack.

"It was nothing," I say softly. "Or I *thought* it was nothing. I blocked a shot—it hurt—" I shake my head. "They always hurt. But this was straight in the—" I swallow and glance down.

Her eyes flick down, following mine, and then come back up. "It was worse this time?"

I remember the pain—it was fucking excruciating, but, "We're used to pushing through the hurt. That's our job. Our reality. It's just…by the time I realized this was something much worse, it was too late to do anything."

"Cam," she whispers.

"The doctor called it torsion. Usually it's only one testicle, but the shot hit in such a way that I was the lucky recipient of it happening to both. Surgery relieved the pain, but the damage was done and—" My eyes burn. "Well, my last test showed that the damage is permanent. I'm sterile."

I fucking hate that word.

Her hand finds mine. "I'm so sorry that happened."

"It was unlucky," I say. "A shit situation and there's no fixing it"—and I've explored *all* options—"so there's no point in being upset that I can't create a family."

Her words are beyond gentle when she says, "But there's more than one way to make a family. You guys taught me that."

"I know."

I fucking *know.*

And I agree—how could I have the upbringing I had and *not* agree? "And I know I'm a selfish prick to even think otherwise. But..." I shake my head because I don't know how to verbalize what exactly has been eating me up inside.

Logic tells me I should be fine.

I'm healthy now. Not in pain. I'm perfectly *fine*. My dick works. Sex is still great. But more importantly, I have people who love me, a stable job, and a great family.

I just can't make kids.

Big fucking deal.

Most bachelors would find that a dream come true.

Fuck whoever I want, whenever I want, and I don't have to worry about a string of baby mamas?

Fucking golden.

It's just...

That's not what I've always wanted—the fucking around, the meaningless relationships, the quiet, lonely house. No matter how hard I try to spin it as it'll all be great, as I try to be happy that the empty bedrooms in my house are awesome guest rooms waiting for my parents, my siblings, my nieces and nephews, I can't lie.

I wanted them to be filled with *my* kids.

Wanted to share that journey with *my* wife. My...*own* family.

Which is totally unfair. I already have a great family.

No, it's not what I dreamed about, not what my parents have, what my siblings have, what my friends are making.

It's not a family of my own.

But it's more than so many people have, including Athena.

"You lost something and you're grieving it."

I jerk my head up, hate the sadness in her eyes.

She survived a nightmare, and I'm worried about some sperm?

Pathetic.

"I'm fine."

Her fingers squeeze. "Except you're *not* fine, are you?" she says, and though it's phrased as a question, her tone is anything but.

"Ats—"

"It's in your head and it's fucking with your life day-to-day and—"

I wince.

She exhales. "And I know exactly what that's like. To want to forget so much, to have the visceral need to keep moving forward, to pretend it doesn't touch you. But"—her fingers flex around mine—"at the end all of that doesn't matter. It still shades every inch of your life."

"My stuff's minor," I say. "This isn't—I mean— I'm lucky, Ats. I get that. Especially after all you went through. I just need to shut up and move on. It's fine. It's like you said—there's more than one way to make a family."

She studies me for a long moment, her dark brown eyes fixed on mine. "It's not a competition for who has the most trauma," she finally says.

"Ats—"

"And I wasn't talking about my past—" She blows out a breath then releases my hand, scooping up both plates and bringing them to the kitchen sink. I watch as she scrubs at them, her movements jerky and ungraceful.

Completely antithesis to all that is Athena.

"You know my upbringing was shit. My parents were…well, not fucking parents, and my mom was vindictive bordering on abusive, something that got worse after she died. I was lucky to get out of that house relatively unscathed—"

Icy shields around her heart and keeping herself distant from everyone who cares about her.

I don't consider that *relatively unscathed*, but…

What the fuck do I know?

"But I got out and I found Lex, found you guys, and my life is better for it."

I hold my breath, wanting to tell her how amazing I think she is, how fucking in love with her I am, but more than that, I need to understand. "So what's shading your life now?"

Because she still has those icy walls and keeps her distance, and the sadness in her…it's only grown in the last year.

She exhales, setting the plates in the drying rack and wiping her hands on a towel.

Her eyes—those gorgeous brown eyes—are filled with such hurt that I want to cross to her, want to tell her that everything will be all right.

But I don't know that.

And I can't even get my own head together, so how in the fuck can I possibly offer up that little tidbit as fact?

"Fuck," she says softly. "I think we both need to get drunk."

"Athena." I move to her.

She turns for the cabinet where I have the booze, pulls out my last bottle of whisky.

"Baby."

Her shoulders hitch up and I know I shouldn't say that, shouldn't step closer, shouldn't wrap my fingers around her wrist and pry the bottle out of her grip. But…I get it now.

I understand.

"This is about Tommy."

The case gone wrong.

When she and Lex were in real danger.

They don't make a habit of discussing their job in front of us, so I usually just hear bits and pieces—unless I'm eavesdropping, of course.

But I heard about Tommy.

About his funeral and his kids and his widow.

"Don't," she whispers.

I stop thinking about all the things I shouldn't do and start doing what I should have years ago.

"Come here," I order, wrapping my arms around her, drawing her against my chest. I smooth a hand over her curls. "I'm so sorry, cupcake."

She exhales, and I don't miss that it's shaky.

So, I hold her a little tighter. "It wasn't your fault."

She lifts her head then, deep brown eyes damp with sadness.

"He died saving me," she whispers. "If it wasn't my fault then whose was it?"

CHAPTER TWELVE

Athena

I REGRET the words the moment they slip out of my mouth.

Stupid to admit them aloud.

That's an inside thought, something that should remain buried.

But once I start, I can't stop.

"He had kids, Cam," I whisper. "And a wife. And—" My voice breaks and I slam my lids closed, hating that I can feel dampness clinging to the bases of my lashes. "I'm me."

He tsks and the sound is so out of Martha's playbook that I still for a moment. But then he's cupping my jaw, tilting my head up. "Open your eyes, cupcake."

I don't like orders.

Or endearments.

But I can't resist him, not like this, not right now, not…well, maybe not *ever*.

And I can't process how dangerous that thought is with his arms around me, his warm spicy scent in my nose, his hard body pressed to mine. Cam is…well, he's not that lanky college kid anymore.

He's a man and—

For better or worse, my body is very aware of that.

"Athena, baby"—he strokes a finger down my cheek—"open your eyes."

And…I do.

I find myself staring into Cam's hazel gaze, lost in the swirling greens and golds and grays. They're beautiful, like an abstract painting I can stare at for hours and hours.

But it's the emotions swirling within his eyes that steal my breath, that stop me from pulling away.

"You've said it before," he tells me gently. "Made it clear you think that your life is less valuable than someone else's because of your upbringing or the woman you've become."

I inhale.

Because I know I do that.

I know that some part of me *feels* that.

"You're a good person."

And though my initial instinct is to demure, to make some joke in order to ignore the feelings that sends spinning through me, I bite it back. I'm not worthless. I do good work. I try my best. I've made something of my life when no one—*no one*—thought that would happen, but—

"Tommy was better," I say softly. "And his family deserved to have him in their lives."

Cam's eyes flash with anger. "And *we* don't deserve to have you?"

My heart leaps, surging up into the back of my throat. "Cam."

"We love you, Ats. You're part of our family—even if sometimes you try not to be."

God. Why does that slice through me?

Because it's true?

I exhale. "I don't try to do it, you know?"

His thumb brushes over my bottom lip. "I know."

"And I'm closer to you guys than I've ever been to anyone in my life."

His eyes soften. "I know that too." He leans in, rests his forehead against mine for a moment. "Same as I know that Lex would have been tearing himself apart if you'd put yourself between him and the bullet. Same as I know that Tommy would have felt the same too. You guys do the job you do because you care about people, and"—he lifts his head, thumb brushing along my bottom lip again—"if Tommy was an asshole, you wouldn't be tearing yourself apart like this."

I still for a second.

Then start laughing.

"What the fuck, Cam?" I say, shoving at his chest.

He grins, and fuck if I don't want to kiss him. To taste that smile. To distract myself from the hurt. To…

Give in.

I can't.

He chuckles, but doesn't let me go, just tugs at a curl. "You know it's true."

I scowl.

He tugs another curl, his smile gentle, his voice soft. "Just like you know as well as I do that someone telling you the truth doesn't make it any easier to bear."

Any trace of amusement fades. "I'm really sorry about your injury."

He touches the back of his knuckles to my cheek, silently acknowledging me. "And I'm really sorry about Tommy."

"I keep hearing my mom's voice in my head," I admit. "The one who took great pleasure in telling me I wasn't worth anything."

"I keep thinking about the empty rooms in my house and how they won't be filled with my kids." He sighs. "And then I hear Coach telling me to pull my fucking weight."

"Dammit," I whisper.

"I know," he mutters. "We're a fucking pair, aren't we?"

"I could really use that whisky now."

He releases me then snags two mugs from the cabinet, picks up the bottle, and pours generously into both of them. "How about I do you one better? Whisky"—he passes over one of the cups—"*and* battling some dragons and orcs?"

———

I GROAN SOFTLY and start to peel open my lids.

Then immediately stop when my head all but screams in protest.

Whisky—far too much of it.

For a second, I just lay prone, eyes closed, waiting for the rolling wave of pain to chill the fuck out. When it eventually does, I move slower this time, slitting them open just the slightest bit.

Ugh. That's not fun.

There's barely any light in the room, but it still jabs at my eyeballs as I try to gain my bearings. There's a ceiling above me, something soft—presumably a bed, if I'm using my superior deductive reasoning skills—below me. Ands there's a faint glimmering of light, as though there's a lamp on in another room.

I'm hot, I suddenly realize, and my back may be cushioned on something soft, but my side is pressed, crammed really, against something rock-solid.

Heat. *Hard.*

My eyes fly open again, and I ignore the jab of pain this time when I realize where I am and—

Who I'm with.

Cam's arms are wrapped tightly around me, one beneath my shoulders, the other around my middle, one big, hot palm resting on my hip.

His breathing is slow and steady and ruffling the hair by my ear.

I struggle to keep my breathing steady, especially with every muscle in my body taut, every instinct telling me to get the fuck out.

Right now.

"Athena."

For a second, I panic, thinking he's awake, thinking he's found me here in his bed, and—

A sigh, his arms tightening, drawing me closer—

Holy fucking shit.

He's hard—and yeah, I know I've thought that already in the last two minutes.

But...he's *hard*.

And pressed into my hip and throbbing and—

I slip free of his hold before I do something stupid. Like reach down, wrap my fingers around his cock, and start stroking.

Sweet baby Jesus.

My headache increases as I stumble away from the bed, mostly because I realize I'm not wearing pants.

Or a shirt—or not *my* shirt.

I'm covered in Cam's tee, the cotton skating over my curves, hanging to mid-thigh. No bra. No underwear. Just...

A shirt.

And he's...

I avert my eyes again.

Naked. No. Okay, *almost* naked. That lickable ass is barely covered in a pair of tiny boxer briefs.

"Athena," he murmurs, and I know I need to get the hell out of here.

The talk last night, drinking and playing video games—I could accept both of those. But waking up like this?

No. Fucking *no*.

I don't bother looking for my clothes, just steal a pair of sweats that I cinch tight around my waist and socks that dwarf my feet from the bag in the corner. I have other stuff in the car, including a jacket. These are just to get me decent. I'll return them another time.

I exhale, slip out into the hall, and move to my shoes by the door. My purse is on the counter, along with my cell, and I snag both after I shove my feet into my boots. Then I'm slipping out into the early morning.

It's still mostly dark, and the rain's falling fast and furiously.

I bleep my car's locks, yank open the door, plunk into the driver's seat, and turn on the engine. A breath to steady myself before I start to back up.

"Fuck!" I hiss, slamming on the brakes, skidding in the wet earth, horror blooming in my middle as I take in the scene captured by the backup camera.

The bridge that spans the river…

Is gone.

CHAPTER THIRTEEN

Cam

A SHOCK of cold wakes me up.

"Jesus Christ," a voice mutters. "Why the fuck do you sleep so deeply?"

I frown, eyes slitting open, wiping a hand over my face, the words belatedly processing. I don't sleep deeply, not normally anyway. But two bottles of whisky and a shit-ton of beer over only a few nights and I'm not exactly running on all cylinders. "I'm up," I mutter, realizing my hand is wet again, that Athena has dumped water on me a second time. "Can you dispense with soaking me and the bed every time it's time to wake up?"

"I would," she grinds out, "if you'd actually *wake up* the first half-dozen times I've tried to rouse you."

I frown, dragging the edge of the sheet over my face and chest and not missing that she watches the movement.

Watches me as though she can't look away.

My heart thuds hard against my rib cage, hope blooming, but it's quickly distinguished because that can't be right—it's the hangover and sleepiness talking.

Oh, and the fact that I've been in love with her for a decade and wanted nothing more than to have her hot gaze dragging over my naked body.

Small details.

And, speaking of small details, the only thing better would be her hands dragging over my naked body…or her tongue.

My dick twitches.

"Cam!"

"I'm up," I rasp.

Too many parts of me are *up*.

"Yeah," she snaps, turning away, my sweats and tee positively dwarfing her frame. "I see that now. But it took ten minutes of me shouting at you *plus* the glass of water to get your ass to stir."

Right.

Well…that sounds annoying. So annoying that I don't have to worry about scarring her with my penis any longer.

I push out of bed, start pulling off the wet blankets. "So," I mutter, "what's lit the fire under your ass at"—I flick my gaze to the clock on my bedside table—"five in the morning?"

"It's still raining," she says, turning for the hall and I see that her shirt is dotted with drops, that I can hear the rain hitting the roof.

Okaaay…

"The weather report said that it'd be a big one," I remind her.

She stills for a moment, her shoulders stiff. "Well, it's a fucking *big one*, that's for sure," she says dryly.

My eyes shoot up.

Was that?

Had she?

I look down at my dick in confusion, see that it's behaving, then shake it off and follow her to the front door, reaching her side just as she wrenches it open.

Immediately, I'm assaulted by wind, and a shock of cold slashes me across my bare torso, but before I can tell her to close it, she's stepping out into the elements and disappearing from sight.

"Shit." I grab my coat from the hook by the door, shove my feet into my boots, and hurry after her.

I don't have to go far. She's standing by my car, staring out at—

"*Fuuuck*," I groan.

Staring out at the river, which is rushing by. Staring out at a tree that's been taken down by the wind or the water, a tree that's currently lying across my bridge.

No lying where my bridge *used* to reside.

It's mostly dark, so I can't see everything, just the skeleton of the foundation, broken pieces of concrete and twisted metal and…

An unpassable gorge between us and the route home.

———

"THANKS, DAN," I say, and hang up.

Then groan and drop my phone on the counter.

"What is it?" Ats asks, the energy inside her coiled like a snake ready to strike. "Is he coming by?"

I rub at a throb in my temple. "No," I say. "They'll need bigger equipment than he can get his hands on right now, especially with the storm still hitting hard." She makes a sound and I lift my head, meet her gaze. "There's flooding all up and down the river. He did promise to come as soon as he's able, but that might be a few—" I hesitate because she's not going to like this.

Not going to like it at all.

"Hours?" she asks hopefully.

"Days," I say quietly.

She's still for a long moment then pushes up out of her chair, cursing softly.

"I'm sorry," I tell her. "If I thought for a moment the bridge would go out, I would have gotten us the hell out of here yesterday."

She plunks her hands on her hips and glances up at the ceiling, quiet for a long moment.

"Ats."

She drops her head back down. "It's not your fault."

"I mean, I'm the one who went rogue and made you come out here." I move close to her, rounding to her front and crouching slightly to meet her eyes. "I know you don't want to be stuck here. I'm sorry, cupcake."

Something flares in her stare and I hold my breath.

But she just sighs again. "Tell me you at least have good junk food."

"You saw the contents of my kitchen," I say gently, tilting my head toward the fridge, the cabinets. "What do *you* think?"

"I think…" An exhale, her nose wrinkling. "I think I'm going to have to go out into the rain and get my backup Car Snacks."

———

"IF I KNEW you were holding out on your mom's cinnamon rolls, I never would have braved the rain."

My mouth twitches as I pull the plate out of the microwave, thankful that I spent a shit-ton of money last summer redoing the electrical to this property. I'd about pissed myself at the cost of burying the power lines and buying the generator, but considering I can still do things like use the microwave and not worry about the food spoiling, I know the work has already paid for itself.

Plus, it's the first time I've seen a smile on Athena's face since she woke me up this morning.

It certainly wasn't there when she was annoyed about it taking forever to rouse me, definitely not when she showed me the bridge, nor when we brought her belongings inside, including those backup Car Snacks.

I put the plate down in front of her. "I'll even offer you some coffee." I pull out the Keurig from a high shelf, and the variety pack of pods. "Pick your poison," I tease as I plug it in. I pull out a mug, take the pod she selects, and start brewing her some caffeine, hoping to keep that smile in place.

And considering the pleasure on her face as she downs my mom's cinnamon roll, I think that's in reach.

I sit down with my own plate and take advantage of studying her while she's distracted.

Curls and cheekbones. Kissable lips and long, thick lashes.

Beautiful. Mysterious. Closed-off.

Except…she hasn't been that, not since she's been here.

Maybe not since that hug on my porch.

I've seen fury and sass. Strength and focus. And…vulnerability, a glimpse behind those icy shields.

"What?" she says, and I realize I've been staring again. Staring so long that I've been caught red-handed.

"Nothing." I quickly cut off a bite and shove it into my mouth.

"Cam," she says on a sigh. "We're stuck here, and I know I've been a grumpy bitch, but I promise to not throw anymore liquids on you."

My lips twitch.

"I wouldn't waste my coffee that way."

I snort.

"So you don't have to keep staring at me like I'm a bug."

"That's not what I'm doing." Well not the bug part, anyway. The staring I'm *definitely* doing.

"No?" she asks. "Then what *are* you doing?"

CHAPTER FOURTEEN

Athena

I SET my fork down onto my clean plate and stare across the table at Cam.

He's been watching me like I'm a cornered animal about to strike—and I can't really blame him. I've given him more than a glimpse of my temper over the last twenty-four hours, and even though the hangry side of me is tamed, I'm still not thrilled to be stuck here.

I need to get back to work.

There are leads to follow up on, and I can't help but feel that I'm getting close to finding out who was really behind the bust gone wrong last year.

That I'm getting close to finding out *who's* behind what happened to Tommy.

But I'm not going to crack the case trapped in the mountains with a hot hockey player.

"Cam?" I press. "What is it? Do I have something on my face?" Cream cheese frosting or cinnamon and butter from scarfing down the delicious baked good?

"No," he says quickly. "And nothing's up."

"Then what? Why are you staring? I meant what I said—I won't waste my coffee by throwing it at you."

He shakes his head, lips turning up at the edges. "It's nothing. I'm just…" He sighs.

"You're what?" I press.

He shoves another bite of cinnamon roll into his mouth. "I should, um, go out and check the generator after I finish eating. Make sure it's gassed up and ready to use if we lose power."

If I'm not mistaken, his cheeks are flushed.

"*Cam.*"

His eyes hit mine. "You don't want to know, Ats. You know you don't."

That sends my pulse skittering. I should leave it alone. I know I should.

But I don't.

"Yes," I say quietly. "I do."

Because some part of me already knows, already feels it. And some part of me *needs* to hear it.

"Athena—"

"Tell me."

He closes his eyes and stares out the window for a long time. "I know you're in love with Lex, so I—"

I nearly knock over my mug. "*What?*"

"—know this makes things complicated." He pushes his bowl away. "But I know you'd never do anything to mess up his relationship with Frankie—"

"*What?*" I know I'm just repeating myself, but what the actual fuck is this man saying?

"You're a good person, Ats. I know that. And—"

"Okay, Cameron Jackson," I snap, slapping my hands on my table and standing. "Stop right there. I am *not* in love with Lex."

He blinks. "You're not?"

"No. *God* no." I shudder. "He tried to kiss me once—years ago when he was drunk and before we were partners. It was—" I shudder, swallow down a gag. "He's literally like a brother to me. Like all of you—"

I stop, unable to finish the sentiment because Cam…

Well, I don't think of him like I do about Lex or Carter or Chance or Caleb or Connor, now do I?

Because I don't think about any of their penises.

Or their asses.

Or how the stubble on their cheeks might feel rubbing along the insides of my thighs.

But Cam…

Well, I woke up in his arms and wanted to roll over and find out…

"I'm not in love with Lex," I repeat firmly. "I never have been. We both knew that early on, Cam."

His gaze locks on to mine and then he slowly slides his chair back, pushes up to his full height.

He seems bigger now, somehow. Taller. Stronger. *More.*

"You're not in love with Lex," he says quietly, and there's a hint of demand in his tone that has me both bristling and… melting.

This is a side of him…well, it's a side of him that I haven't seen before.

And now I'm thinking about his ass again.

And his dick.

"No," I whisper, "I'm not."

He steps closer. "Not in love with any of them?"

I find myself shifting back. "Any of your brothers?"

He nods, takes another step.

I shake my head. "No," I whisper, sliding another pace away. "I'm not in love with any of the Jacksons."

That has his brows dragging together, a scowl clouding his face. "Well, I am."

"Y-you are?" I ask, sliding back another step, finding my back pressed to the wall, shock rippling through me. He's—

"You're?" I ask incredulously. "With Lex—?"

"No." His mouth curves.

"I-I don't understand."

He cups my jaw, fingertips slightly rough, thumb brushing along my cheek. "I'm in love with you, cupcake."

CHAPTER FIFTEEN

Cam

HER FACE TELLS ME ENOUGH—SHOCK and horror.

The little Jackson brother declaring his feelings.

Fucking stupid.

Fucking—

One second, I'm cupping her cheek, her body close and tempting, filled with so much longing that it's eating me up inside.

And the next…

She's shifting, plastering her body against mine, lifting on tiptoe and wrapping a leg around my waist.

"Wh—"

Her mouth hits mine.

For a blip, I'm frozen in surprise, my mind trying to process with what the actual fuck is going on. Then I realize that it doesn't really matter. Because Athena's kissing me and I'm just standing here, squandering the moment.

That, more than anything, spurs me into action.

Seize the moment.

Take what I can before it's gone.

I step forward, pinning her between my body and the wall, slipping a hand beneath her other leg and hefting her up, coaxing her to wrap it around my waist. She does and we both groan at the contact—my dick, hard and ready, pressed against the softness between her thighs.

"Jesus," she moans, breaking the kiss, "but you've got a big cock, Cam."

All the blood rushes from my head to...well, to my other head.

"And you've got a dirty mouth," I growl, cupping her chin, turning her face back to mine.

"Yeah. So?"

I lean a little closer. "So, let me taste it again."

I don't wait for her to respond, just lower my mouth to hers, taking advantage of her parted lips to slip my tongue inside, to taste her fully. Her moan rumbles up the back of her throat, dances over into my mouth, and she arches against me, riding the hard edge of my cock and making feel like I'm a teenager about to come in my pants.

Christ, that's good.

I press her against the wall, drag my hand up along her side, desperate to feel her bare skin beneath my T-shirt, desperate to have her naked.

And she makes it clear she feels the same, hands scrabbling at my clothes, fingers grasping the hem of my tee and yanking it up.

Yeah, this isn't working for me.

I need horizontal.

I need naked.

I need *Athena.*

Spinning us, I stride to the counter, plunking her onto the edge and reaching for her shirt, but our hands tangle as she reaches for mine at the same time.

She swats at me. "Stop it."

"I'm trying to get you naked," I growl.

"I'm trying to get *you* naked," she counters.

"I think we'll both like you naked more." Oh the things I've dreamed about doing to her. The things I'm *going* to do to her.

"That's debatable," she grumbles but lifts her arms, allows me to tug her shirt up and over her head. "Especially since I've seen *you* naked."

She's not wearing a bra and the sight of her glorious tits bouncing, her pink-tipped nipples hardening beneath my gaze, means that it takes me a minute to process what she's just said. "When have you seen me naked?"

"Yes—" She hisses out a breath as I settle my hands on her waist and start slowly dragging them up along her sides, tracing them forward over the smooth skin of her abdomen. "—terday."

"When?"

"When I woke you up."

"When you tried to drown me, you mean," I tease, sliding them a little higher, drifting them in a little closer. Six inches from the motherland. Two. One. A half.

"I was not—" Her breath hitches when I allow my hands to shift higher, to cup her breasts. "I wasn't trying to drown you," she groans, grabbing my wrists and pressing my hands to her, placing her palms on my fingers, coaxing me to squeeze her tits.

Okay, fine. She doesn't have to coax much.

I'm already massaging those lush curves, feeling the hardened bud of her nipples on my palm, listening to the soft inhales of her breath. "No?" I ask, barely able to hold the thread of conversation. "Sure felt like it."

"It's not my fault"—I roll her nipple between my thumb and forefinger, revel in the soft moan that escapes her lips—"that I'm a heavy sleeper."

"It sure—*oh God!*—fucking is."

My lips twitch as I pinch a little harder. "Is *not*."

Hot brown eyes on mine. "Is—" I lean down and suck one of those pink buds into my mouth. "To," she finishes on a hiss.

The fact that we're arguing while I'm actively touching—

finally touching—this gorgeous woman's body isn't lost on me, but I can't seem to stop.

Same as I can't stop myself from whispering, "Is not," just before I close my lips around that sensitive bud and suck.

"Is—" She groans, her head falling back against the cabinets. "To."

"Is—" But then she shocks the shit out of me because she's suddenly shoving me backward, dropping to her knees in front of me, and—

"Oh *fuck*," I groan, my knees going week. It takes every bit of focus to keep them locked so I don't collapse and take her down alongside me. "Ats. Oh *fuck*."

Her tongue is...fucking sin personified, and the hint of teeth makes me shiver and groan again when she runs them along my shaft, taking me deep, so deep that I bump the back of her throat. Then she starts working me with her hand, and the tight grip, the suction, the lips and teeth and tongue—

Right.

This isn't going to work for me.

I mean, it's *working*.

Just too well, and this is Athena. *My* Athena. Fuck if I'm going to let her give me all the pleasure.

Reaching down, I hook my hands under her armpits and tug, pulling her off my cock with a soft *pop*.

"Hey!" she protests, reaching for me again.

But I've got some moves of my own and I execute them quickly, reaching for the hem of her stolen sweats, pushing them down, exposing—

"*Fuck*," I grit out.

"What?" she whispers.

"You're gorgeous everywhere."

Half of her mouth quirks up. "And this is a problem?"

"It's a problem for my self-control," I grumble.

"Well, considering I don't want you *in* control," she

murmurs, stroking a hand down my chest, cupping my dick again, "I don't see how that's a problem."

I snag her wrist, press a kiss to her palm.

Tempting.

Fucking tempting to completely let go and fuck her like an animal.

But…this is Athena.

I've dreamed about being with her, tasting her, touching her, kissing her, *fucking* her for near on a decade.

I don't know if I'll get another chance, don't know if those icy walls will snap down again and try to close me out. So…I need to take my time, to worship her like she deserves.

And if those walls *do* close?

Well, fuck the ice. I'm breaking out my chisel. Or blowtorch.

Or fucking *flamethrower*.

Because this woman, who I've loved for years, is going to be mine.

I inhale, grasp tight to my control, and I *move*.

Lifting her up onto the counter again, kissing her deeply, tasting her squeak on my tongue, presumably from the cold counter—or maybe because I've snaked my hand down, slipped it between her legs and stroked through the slick folds of her pussy.

I don't stop though, especially when she parts her thighs and gives me better access.

Fuck yes.

I break the kiss, drag my lips along her jaw, down her throat, nipping at the sensitive spot that makes her shiver.

Then I keep going, kissing at the tops of her breasts, closing my lips around one taut nipple and sucking.

Her hands dive into my hair and clench tight, sending pain rippling across my scalp. It doesn't bother me, though. If anything, that red haze of pain wraps its fingers around my cock and strokes furiously, sending me even closer to the edge, closer to the point of no return.

But I just keep moving down, keep focusing on Athena.

On her soft skin. On her slick pussy as I kiss my way down her belly and position myself between her thighs. On that tight grip of my hair and the soft curve of her hips. On her moans in my ears and her scent in my nose…

And her taste on my tongue.

"Cam," she cries, her grip on my hair not loosening, her hips bucking, her head falling back to hit against the cabinets again.

Yeah, *that's* not going to work for me either.

CHAPTER SIXTEEN

Athena

One moment, I'm enjoying the feel of his tongue stroking over my clit and the next I've lost his touch, his heat, that glorious tongue and those perfectly roughened fingertips.

"Cam!" I protest when he pulls back.

But I don't get more than that out because then he's scooping me off the counter, holding me close, gaze scanning.

"What—"

He strides across the room and kicks the table to the side. It slides off the rug like it weighs no more than a bag of feathers, hitting the wall with a *thunk*.

"I—"

He drops to his knees with me in his arms and though I expect him to pin me to that fluffy rug, to spread my thighs and fuck me hard and fast, he doesn't. Instead, *he* leans back, taking me with him, settling me on top.

Yeah. Okay. I can work with this.

But then his hands drop to the insides of my thighs and he starts drawing me up his body.

I frown.

Then…I grin.

"Cameron Jackson," I mock-scold. "Are you trying to get me to do something naughty?"

Like ride his face until I come.

Yeah, I can definitely work with that.

"Get up here," he orders, desire blazing in his hazel eyes, the words a rough order, "where it's nice and warm."

I shiver at the rasp, at the demand, while at the same time that kernel of warmth hidden deep in my heart, a kernel that had once only been fueled by Lex, then Martha, then the other Jacksons…

Cam has always been there.

But now he's throwing gasoline on the spark, sending it flaming to life inside me.

Warmth flows through my belly.

He knew the counter was cold.

And now we're on a rug…with him taking the brunt of the cool fabric, the hard floor, and me…

Getting to enjoy the heat of his body—

And his mouth.

Because he keeps coaxing and now I've slid up his torso, over his chest, his neck…to settle on his face.

He groans and the sound vibrates through me, but even as I'm absorbing that sensation—reveling in it—his hands settle on my ass, and…

His tongue gets to work.

Stroking through me, circling my clit. Joining in tandem with the stubble on his jaw, his lips to drive me crazy.

One hand lifts, cupping my breast, pinching my nipple, and I gasp, my hips jerking.

He stills and for a second, I worry that I've hurt him. But *only* for a second, because then his tongue begins to work my pussy with furious intent and his fingers roll my nipple, and his free hand palms my ass, kneading the flesh, encouraging me to continue rocking against his face.

To continue *riding* his face.

I jerk when I feel it—the first licks of an orgasm teasing through me.

Flames scorching my toes, crawling up my calves, my thighs. Creeping up my fingers, my arms, along my collarbones, over my breasts, down my belly…

And meeting between my thighs.

"Oh God," I whisper, still rocking, still grinding my pussy on his face.

"Come for me, cupcake," he orders gruffly, the words muffled…because I'm doing my best to smother him.

It's right there—my orgasm teasing me, hanging just on the edges of sensation, so close, so near, but…just not enough.

And thank fuck he sees that.

Thank fuck he doesn't stop and ask me what to do. He just takes action—to glorious, pleasurable results.

He shifts me a little higher and fucks me with his tongue.

"I—" I throw my head back, still grinding, still taking advantage of that stubble on his cheeks, but now, with the added motion of his tongue, filling me, fucking me, I'm plummeting over the edge.

"Cam," I moan, hips jerking, orgasm rippling through me.

He groans, tongue still working me, hands still on my ass and breasts, drawing out my pleasure until my head goes fuzzy and my limbs lax and—

I squeak as he flips us, as my back hits the rug.

Cam doesn't crawl on top as I half-expect, as I half-hope.

Instead, he stays between my legs, and he doesn't stop fucking my pussy with his tongue.

Only this time, his hand joins in on the party, his thumb circling my clit, a finger sliding deep. Then another. And—

"Cam!" I hiss.

"You like it," he murmurs against my labia, nipping lightly at my flesh and sending me shivering all over again. "And you need it, cupcake. Need to be ready for me to fuck you."

I want to make a quip about his big dick, or about being more than ready for him to stretch me to overfull, but I don't get the chance because he drops his head again and then he's driving his fingers into me, he's sucking at my clit, he's sending another orgasm barreling down on me, and—

"Oh God!"

I come apart, shattering into a hundred pieces that he manages to corral, to keep together as he crawls up my body and cradles me close. My chest is heaving, my eyes are half-mast. But I can feel his cock throbbing against my hip, calling to that aching emptiness inside me. I know I could stop here, could leave this alone, could take my orgasms, chalk this whole interaction up to insanity, wait for us to get sprung from river jail, and go back to my life.

But that would be pretending.

Hiding from a fact I already knew in my heart since that night a decade ago when he first said I was beautiful.

Cam has feelings for me.

I don't think it's love—he doesn't know me, not really. But it's definitely lust, definitely *like*. And...I have those feelings too. And...

Well, once he gets to know me, the so-called love will calm, the crush will fade. We'll be able to enjoy each other's bodies until we don't any longer.

It'll be mutually beneficial. Pleasure for both of us and then... moving forward—Cam toward some nice girl who'll recognize that family doesn't mean sharing DNA, me toward a case I'll be able to take on with a level head.

Because Cam is right.

Tommy may have given his life for mine, but I would have done the same given the chance, and I'm going to make sure his sacrifice is worth something.

I inhale, feel that fact settle deep inside.

Then I tuck it away.

Enough of that right now.

Enough of anything except Cam and I and the pleasure we can bring each other—or the pleasure I'm going to bring *him* because he's done an exemplary job of pleasuring *me*.

He's tracing circles on my belly, random patterns that raise goose flesh on my skin, that wake my nerves, start building heat between my legs. But he doesn't show any urgency to climb atop me and fuck me.

Patient.

A gentleman.

Not rushing. Pleasuring me first. Looking after me.

I inhale because that settles deep, right next to my grief for Tommy, the way I feel about Lex and Martha and the rest of the Jacksons, including Cam.

Though Cam…

Well, he's the only Jackson I want to fuck.

The only Jackson I'm *going* to fuck.

I brush his hand away, push at his chest.

He doesn't move, though he looks up at me, our gazes connecting. "Something you're trying to tell me, cupcake?" he asks quietly, his lips twitching. He settles his hand back on my side, his big, warm palm spanning my waist, his fingers dipping south, brushing *oh so slowly* close to—

I snag his wrist.

As much as I'm okay with him working me with those magic fingers, I need to take charge of this, need him to be pleasured and looked after and taken care of too.

Ignoring the blip of alarm that raises in me, I push at his chest again, roll him to his back, and clamber atop that hard, hot body.

Time to focus on something—*anything*—else.

And luckily, his smile grows.

"Something you want to *ride*, baby?"

CHAPTER SEVENTEEN

Cam

I KNOW by the smile on her face that I'm in way over my head.

And I can't give a fuck.

So, I don't fight her as she pushes me back onto the rug, don't argue when she climbs on top of me, when the slick, swollen folds of her pussy brush at my cock.

"Condom?" she asks, slowly lowering herself, rubbing against me, driving me crazy with the wet heat I'm desperate to fuck.

I want to tell her to forget it, that I'm clean, that I can't get her pregnant.

But that isn't a conversation for now, isn't something to decide in the heat of the moment. So, I make a herculean effort to reach up onto the narrow row of shelves, snag my wallet, and pull out the condom that I keep inside.

"Jackpot," she whispers, tearing the packet open with her teeth and holding it up like it's the best prize ever.

And then she's rolling it down the length of my cock, making me see stars. I bite back my groan, the urge to flip her and drive deep and fast into that tight, wet cunt. I'm sweating and my hands are shaking, and my control is razor thin by the time she sits back on her heels and smiles at me.

Fuck.

That self-satisfied smirk isn't helping.

Not when she's so fucking beautiful, so confident, so ready to take exactly what she wants.

"Teasing?" I rasp when she circles the base of my cock, her cool fingers stroking the bare skin beneath the edge of the condom.

"Appreciating," she says. "Knowing that I need to get my mouth on this gorgeous dick again. Knowing that I need to feel you coming down my throat."

Fuck.

"Cupcake," I warn.

Her smirk grows and she leans in, brushing her nose against mine. "I'll get you to explain that nickname." A press of her lips against mine. "But later. Right now"—she straddles my waist again, rests her palms by my shoulders—"I need you inside."

I open my mouth, but I don't get anything out except for a groan because she's notching the head of my cock at her entrance, shifting her hips, and—

"*Fuck*," I groan.

But she's right there with me, hissing out a breath as she takes me to the hilt, her moan filling the air, her pussy clamping tightly around me.

It's intoxicating and dangerous, and I'm desperate to buck up into her, to grasp her waist, to take over.

It would be great.

But *this* is better, watching her face change as she takes me deep, watching her eyes glaze with pleasure, watching her tits bounce as she rides me faster, rides me harder.

"That's it, baby," I coax. "Rock those hips. Take me deep. Fuck me hard."

"Cam," she whispers. "I—"

I hear it in her voice, know exactly what she needs now that I've tasted her and touched her and been inside her.

She needs *more*.

I reach down and slip my hand between us, locating that sensitive bundle of nerves at the top of her cunt, stroking my thumb over her clit with no quarter—

"*Cam!*"

Yeah, that's it.

She moves faster, grinding down onto me, her pussy clamping tight, so tight that I can feel my orgasm hovering, knowing that I need to get her there before I fucking blow.

I circle her clit, press more firmly, can't resist gripping one hip and grinding up into her as she strokes down.

"Oh," she whispers, her head falling back, her rhythm faltering.

So, I do it again. And then again.

And then—

"Fuck," she moans.

I feel it, the flutters of her pussy, the orgasm rippling through her, and the taut rhythmic squeezing of my cock fractures the last bit of my control.

I come apart, thrusting up into her, knowing I'm groaning way too loud, but not giving a fuck as I come harder than I've ever come before.

My vision hazes. My nerves are on fire. I grind deep once, twice, maybe a *hundred* times more before I go limp, every part of my body lax and heavy.

"Jesus Christ," she mutters what might have been minutes or hours later.

"Seriously," I manage to say, though the words sound slurred, like I'm drunk. "That was insane."

She's slumped against my chest, her face pressed into my shoulder. "Yes. *That.*" She lifts up enough to meet my eyes. "We can just stay right here for the next ten hours right?"

Then she's dropping her head back down, her cheek against

my chest, her breath teasing my skin, her arms and legs limp—
though there is *one* thing that's still tense.

That pussy of hers is still holding tightly onto my dick.

Which is why I don't care about the storm outside.

Nor the bridge destroyed by the river.

Or the possibility that the generator might not do its job.

Or what will happen when we get out of here.

I just wrap my arms around her and hold her close.

"Yeah, cupcake. We can stay right here."

———

"JESUS CHRIST," I hear as I stand next to the river bank, trying to figure out if there's a way to get across without drowning.

I turn and see Athena has picked her way across the mud pit that was my yard. She pauses at my side, staring out at the water.

"I don't think I've ever seen water move that fast."

I shift a little closer, needing to touch her even though it's been barely ten minutes since I peeled myself away from her gorgeous body. When my shoulder brushes hers, she glances away from the roaring river and up at me, eyes soft in a way that makes me want to claim her forever.

"Snow melt plus storm," I say, giving into the urge to slip my arm around her shoulders and draw her a little closer. I hold my breath, half expecting her to pull away, but relief pours through me when she stays close.

Though that's probably because she's shivering.

Speaking of which, I turn us, start guiding her back to the house.

"Should we try to find a way out of here?" she asks quietly. "If the river keeps rising—"

"It's expected to crest in the next hour," I say, pushing the door open and drawing us inside. "We have power and cell service. Yeah, we'll keep an eye on the water height, but the safest place right now is staying put until we get the all clear."

"Hmm." She scowls.

"What?"

Her nose wrinkles and it's fucking adorable. "Why are you being reasonable?"

"Are you that much of a workaholic that you can't take the weekend off?" I counter. "It's Saturday. Hopefully tomorrow the roads will be clear enough that we can make a plan."

"And come Monday?" she asks, not addressing the fact that we both know is true—she *is* a workaholic and would happily be in the office all weekend, even if she wasn't doubly focused because of what happened with Tommy.

"You have your laptop?" I ask.

She just shoots me a droll look, as though to say, *Do I have my head?*

"You have your laptop," I say dryly. "Work the weekend if you need to. Kill some orcs with me and eat junk food if you don't. And come Monday, hopefully we'll be able to get out of here—"

"Hopefully?" An arch question.

"At the very least, we should be able to get across the river, hitch a ride to town, and rent a car to drive home, yeah? As soon as I get the bridge fixed"—or more likely, buy a prefab replacement bridge and have to pay more than this cabin cost to get it installed, but…that's life being lifey, especially after this season ended like it did—"I'll get your car back to you."

Her expression sobers. "What?"

I frown. "What do you mean *what?* I'll get you back to the Bay, cupcake."

"I know you will." She shifts to fully face me. "But all of a sudden you've got shadows in your eyes, Cam. Is this about"—her eyes flick down—"because injury or not, DNA-contributing-ability or not, you were incredible."

Not gonna lie, that feels good.

Also…not gonna lie, I can't pretend I don't know what she's hinting at.

"I'm…" I sigh. "It's not that I can't have kids biologically." Then add as she opens her mouth, protest in those big brown eyes, "I feel that deeply," I whisper. "And I know I'm just starting to deal with it. But…" I sigh again. "What's hard to let go of is Coach's bullshit and how the end of the season went. I didn't have my head in the game, and it wasn't pretty. And I know I'm going to have to start training soon, so it won't be long before I'm on the ice and dealing with him and Pat and the other assholes again. I need to do better, need to make sure I'm pulling my weight, need to make sure there's nothing that can rattle me."

Her brows drag together. "Didn't you have, like, the most points last season of your entire career?"

I still, something like hope in my veins before I shove it down. "Yeah, but it doesn't really matter."

Now her eyebrows flick up. "Gonna clue me in why?"

"We lost in the first round of the playoffs, Ats. And I know I directly caused at least one goal and thus one loss. It's just fact."

"And what were the other twenty-odd dudes on the team doing?"

I still.

"Exactly," she says triumphantly.

I scowl.

"You're not alone on the ice," she presses. "And even if you were, sometimes shit happens and things go wrong, and you can't blame…"

She trails off, probably realizing that this advice should apply to the both of us.

"Damn," she whispers a moment later.

"It's good advice," I say. "But easy to give and hard to accept."

Her nose wrinkles. "Ugh."

Grinning, I snag one of the bags of junk food she brought in. "Car Snack?"

"*Now* you're getting it," she says reaching inside and pulling out a bag of gummy bears. She tears open the top, starts shoving them by the handful into her mouth.

"Gonna run out of Car Snacks you keep going like that," I point out.

A shrug. "I'll call into the office."

I lift my brows in question.

"Request some drones to deliver us better snacks."

"*Better* than Car Snacks?"

"Well, these would be Trapped by a Flooded River Snacks, so they'd clearly be superior."

I snort. "And the full cupboards and bags of food you brought in aren't enough?"

"One," she ticks off on her fingers, "those full cupboards are packed with healthy crap—"

I chuckle.

"And two, I was anticipating a four hour drive, not being trapped with a ravenous hockey player with an affection for Snickers—"

I had, in fact, devoured the king-sized Snickers from the bag. But still, there are *four* full bags of snacks. The thought of going through that much junk food in the next two days is…

Well, not impossible because we can both *eat.*

But certainly improbable.

"—if I had anticipated having to fill your hollow Jackson leg, I would have brought twice as much."

I laugh and shake my head. "I'm scared to think what you'd bring on a road trip."

Her eyes dance. "Why's that?"

"Because you wouldn't have room for clothes."

"*I* happen to think"—she slides her gaze down my body and

I feel heat flicker in my stomach, feel that flicker grow into a full-on inferno when she steps close and drags her hand across my chest, down my torso, slips it under the waistband of my sweats to grasp my cock—"that clothes are highly overrated."

CHAPTER EIGHTEEN

Athena

"No." I scowl and throw up my hands. "Jesus Christ, Cam! How the hell am I supposed to do this?"

He's fighting a smile, which makes me want to launch the controller at him. "I don't know how it's possible, but you're actually better at video games when you're drunk."

"Ugh." I toss the controller to the side. "I hate that you're right." I scowl at him again for good measure. "And I hate even more that you don't have any additional bottles of whisky so that I can kick this boss's ass."

He takes the controllers and sets them aside. "Who knew that a double jump would be your downfall?"

Double ugh.

I just can't get the timing right, which is frustrating. I'm not a professional athlete, but I know how to handle myself. That I can't hit two buttons at the correct moment is infuriating. "I need more junk food."

Grinning, he passes me the bag, which, thankfully, still has plenty of my favorites. I pull out a bag of gummy worms and start taking my frustrations out by biting their tiny heads off.

We've spent the last few hours playing this game—after fucking for the hours in between watching the river rise, crest, and begin to descend, and then hitting the kitchen ravenous.

Thankfully, Cam has a metric ton of cinnamon rolls in his freezer, along with casseroles and pasta sauce that Martha clearly stocked up for him, so there's no chance of starving—

Or, God forbid, having to eat more of the vegetables in the fridge.

He pushes up from the couch and disappears into the hall. I have to bite back my question, have to resist the urge to stop him from leaving. A dangerous thought, that, being so in tune with him that I want to know where he's going and what he's doing and…

Why he's leaving me.

That has panic ramping, almost sending me from the couch and out into the darkness. I'll channel my inner mountain goat and leap rock-to-rock then hitchhike the four hours back down to the Bay.

This is dumb.

This is stupid.

This is…going to leave me bloody and bruised and—

I'm sure to fuck it up and then I'll lose everything.

Every*one*—

Fuck, I need to go.

"Come with me?"

I blink and turn to see that Cam's back, wearing his coat and boots. He has my jacket in his hands and *my* boots tucked beneath his arm.

There's a wariness in his eyes, as though he knows what I'm thinking, or…maybe that he's feeling nervous too.

Surprisingly, that makes me feel better.

And angry, I guess.

He's not the one who's guaranteed to fuck this up—he's a Jackson, he's a pro at interpersonal relationships. *I'm* the idiot in this scenario. He's…well he's fucking perfect.

"I'm not," he says.

Stilling, I look from the coat back up to his face. "What?"

"You're thinking I have it together, that I know what I'm doing. And you're thinking about bolting the hell out of here because you're scared."

"You said you love me, Cam," I blurt. "That's scary shit."

A ripple of pain across his face, and I kick myself. Fucking it up already. Saying the wrong thing.

They'll never love you. You're unlovable.

I close my eyes.

Warm fingers brush my cheek, and I jerk them open, see that he's crouching in front of me.

"I'm sorry," I whisper.

"It's scary," he whispers back. "Some idiot guy blurting out big emotions when you prefer to keep your distance."

"You can't love me," I say, still whispering. "You don't even know me."

He sighs softly. "I love you, Ats, but you're right. I don't know you, not really. Not all the knowledge that comes from being in a relationship with someone. I don't know all of what's going in here"—he taps my temple—"or here"—the spot above my heart—"but I *do* know the person you are. I knew it from that first time you showed up at my parent's lake house and I know you now. I love that you care about our family, love that you're so passionate about your job and work so hard. I love that you're smart as hell and can protect yourself. I love that you have no qualms about jumping in to battle dragons and orcs and that you don't know a thing about hockey, but you've always cheered me on."

"Hey," I attempt to joke. "I know what icing is now."

"In hockey?" he asks lightly. "Or on my mom's cinnamon rolls?"

Surprised, I laugh.

His fingers trace my lips, my smile, and I feel some pieces

shift inside me—realigning, opening up...*melting*. "Beautiful," he murmurs.

"I don't know what to do with this. I—" I exhale. "I don't know what I'm feeling or thinking, except to know that I'm going to mess it up."

"So...you mess it up," he says, like it's the simplest thing in the world. "And then we figure out a way to fix it." His brows slide together, forming a deep V between them, and I fucking hate that I get to watch the doubt creeping into his eyes in real time. "Of course, that's if you *want* to fix it, if you want to continue this when we, um, get out of here."

It's probably the most reckless thing I've ever done—

Leaning in and cupping his face in my hands when I should pull back, should tell him that, yes, this is all a mistake, should do anything but allow another thread to connect us.

But...

I love him too.

Maybe not the same way as he says he does me—but I love his drive and focus, and the way he's so kind and thoughtful. I love that he didn't bat an eye when his family invaded or when I was a snarly beast waking him up with that splash of water. I love that I've known him for a decade, and he's always been himself.

So, I can't turn away right now, even though I'm quaking in my boots.

"I don't know what I'm doing, or how to...do *this*."

His expression locks down.

"But..." I'm feeling so much—too much and not enough—addicted and unable to stop, terrified to traipse down this trail and yet even more scared to stop. And all of that fuels my next words. "But...I'm willing to try."

Relief across the handsome lines of his face.

And I know that even though this might all blow up in my face...

I still made the right decision.

Of course, I won't know until later, that this will also be the worst mistake of my life.

CHAPTER NINETEEN

Cam

I'm riding high as she lets me help her into her coat, as she sits on the couch and shoves her feet into her boots, as she lets me take her hand and draw her outside.

The sun is setting, and I need to show her why I bought this place.

Need.

Yeah.

To her credit, she doesn't question me, just walks by my side as we pick our way across my yard. The gravel path is riddled with puddles, the rocks scattered this way and that from the storm, but it's traversable and pretty soon we make it to the clearing at the back of my property.

Her exhale tells me enough.

Because it tells me that she feels it too.

"It's why I put an offer in on this place, even though the cabin's walls were practically crumbling down," I say, clambering on top of the boulder and extending my hand.

She hesitates for a moment before taking it, before allowing me to draw her up next to me. "This is beautiful," she says on a sigh, settling by my side and staring out at the valley that sits between me and my neighbor. The sun is setting in the distance, turning the sky into a watercolor of reds and pinks and oranges.

"It is," I agree, slipping an arm around her shoulders.

"But"—she glances up at me, lips twitching—"you bought a house for a view?"

"Well, it certainly wasn't for the house."

Her brows flick up.

"I bought this place from the old owner," I explain, "and the fact that the bridge washed away probably speaks to the state of the property when I first started working on it." I shake my head. "Total shambles—a leaking roof, a rotten floor in the bathroom, electrical that needed replacing, and a septic tank that was pretty much a hazardous waste site."

"Yikes."

"I think the owner was so thrilled to have an offer that he couldn't get out of here fast enough. And my realtor advised… well pretty much against everything to do with this place. But —" I nod out at the valley again.

"But this," she whispers.

"This," I agree, and we stare out at the view for long moments before she speaks again.

"It's clearly not in shambles now."

"No. But it took almost two years."

She glances at me and I see those brows have shot up again.

"I did a lot of work myself." Higher now, and I shrug. "I tore it down to the studs over one off-season, fixed plenty of dry rot, and then spent the next season and then off-season building it back up."

"That's really awesome."

"Though, I did have help with the electrical, plumbing, and the septic tank." I wink at her. "I can handle a piece of tile that's not perfectly level, but a toilet that doesn't flush or a light switch that tries to electrocute me? Not so much."

She grins. "Yeah, I'll take a no on the fire hazards as well."

"Exactly. But, all in all, it was a great project. I learned a lot, cursed a lot, and now I have a great place up here."

"Wow," she says, shaking her head. "How did I not know this?"

"If you knew that Mom stocked my freezer with cinnamon rolls, I'd lose my stash."

Laughter fills the air, and for a moment I feel a hundred feet tall. But then she exhales and hits me with those deep brown eyes. "No really, Cam. Why didn't I know?"

And there's no way I can't give her the truth, though I try to give her the most glossed over version. "I'm good at keeping stuff against my chest until I'm ready to share."

That has her tilting her head to the side, studying me closely. Then her mouth twitches. "Yeah, I'd say so." A beat. "*Ten* years of saying so."

"This is you making a joke about emotions?"

Her mouth twitches again. "It's out there already. If I can't make a joke, I'll run screaming for the hills."

"Thanks," I say dryly

Her face changes. "I didn't mean—"

I bump my shoulder against hers. "I know. I'm teasing."

But there's still sadness in her eyes. "I don't know how to do this, Cam. I'm…well…I'm afraid that there are things inside me that are broken permanently."

"I think you're selling yourself short."

"*I* think you're not looking at this with a clear head." She clenches her hand into a fist, taps it against her thigh. "I'm dangerous. I—"

I take her fingers, carefully release them from the taut grip. "Look, I shared something with you that I haven't told anyone, and you came to me with compassion and understanding—"

"And whisky."

I tug a lock of her hair, well aware she's using the joke to put distance between us. "*And* whisky. But before the whisky," I say, "you listened. You listened and then you shared, cupcake. About yourself. Which I know isn't easy for you."

She exhales.

"If that's not knowing how to do this then I don't know what is."

She falls silent for a long moment, staring out at the setting sun. Wind is rustling through the pine needles and the temperature is dropping, but the water is trending the right way and if we can finagle a ride out of here tomorrow then we'll be back to reality.

Back to normal.

That has a spot between my shoulders tensing.

But I force it to relax.

She sees me know. She knows it all.

And she's still here.

Fine. I know the river is playing a small part of that, but…

It doesn't matter.

Fuck if I'm going to let her go.

I just…well, I just need to make her fall in love with me before we go back to reality.

So, that's why I don't push when she hops off the rock, takes my hand…

And leads me back inside.

Back into the bedroom.

I'm not giving up.

I'll win her heart—

One way or another.

———

"WHAT DO YOU THINK?" I ask the next morning.

Dan shakes his head across the ravine, but it's his voice I hear through my phone pressed to my ear. "Fucked royally. You'll need a whole new bridge."

Considering that half of it washed away and the other half is pinned to the rocky bed by a big ass tree, this isn't a surprise.

But I still hear cash register sounds in my head.

Cha-ching. Cha-ching. Cha-ching!

"How long will that take?"

His pause is long enough that I tense before I bite out, *"Dan."*

"We can put in a temporary one to get the cars out—though it'll take a couple of weeks." A sigh that vibrates through the speaker. "But one that'll pass inspection and last you? Months."

I drop my head back, stare up at the sky.

Bright without a cloud marring blue—no sign of the freak summer rainstorm.

No sign of a summer in my cabin to lick my wounds and come back stronger.

"Okay, well can we start working toward that?"

A nod. "Sure thing. Still need a ride to town?"

I glance down at the river, watch him do the same. "When do you think it'll be safe to get across?"

"Tomorrow?"

Monday. Back to reality.

Back to normal.

Back to…

I flick my gaze to Athena, who's sitting on the porch, feet up on the railing, laptop open, brow furrowed in concentration, and…

I know I need a little more time.

I turn away say quietly, "Tuesday?"

There's a flash of white on the other side of the riverbank and I hear the amusement in his voice when Dan replies. "Have a call out here Wednesday afternoon. That work for you?"

I grin.

Best wingman ever.

CHAPTER TWENTY

Athena

I DIDN'T KNOW it was possible to have this much sex. It's glorious.

And yes, I'm sore.

"Here you go, cupcake," Cam murmurs, leaning in to settle a plate in front of me. A steaming hot cinnamon roll is on it—of course—but this time he's added fruit.

"Trying to corrupt me?"

He kisses the top of my head. "I like you corrupt."

"Considering what you did to me this morning to wake me up, I think *you're* the corrupt one."

A chuckle. "Well, eat your fruit and you *too* can be corrupt."

I grin, shake my head, but pick up a slice of apple and start chomping. "Happy?"

"If you're happy," he murmurs, sitting next to me and settling one big warm palm on my thigh. My pussy clenches, remembering the pleasure that hand can give me, but my heart clenches harder.

I *am* happy.

Which makes the panic inside me grow, threatening to send me mountain-goating across the river.

I take a breath, manage to I shove it down, to inhale, exhale, and just…

Well, fuck, why *can't* I just be happy for the moment?

My phone buzzes on that thought and I glance down, see a familiar number on the screen.

Not work—because when I wasn't being fucked into oblivion the last few days, I've been glued to my laptop and liaising with my team and working my way through a bunch of new data and financial records that just came in.

It doesn't make sense, but I'm getting closer.

I squeeze the side of my phone, stopping the buzzing, but when Cam says, "I'll step out so you can answer that," something inside me shifts.

He knows that work stuff is confidential, that I can't talk freely with someone not on the case.

But he doesn't know who's on the other end of the call.

And…I want to take the universe's sign—my past coming in to remind me of all the things I can't do—and back the fuck up, distance myself from this vulnerability.

Want to avoid, fucking *avoid* all of this shit.

Only, I don't want to lose the warm hand on my thigh, the gentle man at my side. I want to eat my cinnamon roll while it's hot and joke about choking down the "healthy" apple slices.

So…I snag his wrist, hold him in place, and then I swipe a finger across the screen, hit the button for speaker.

It takes a second for the call to connect, but then it does, the background noise telling me enough.

She's up to her usual antics.

"Hi, Mom," I say quietly and feel Cam jerk next to me, feel his gaze searching out mine.

But I just keep my eyes on my phone and exhale.

"I need some money."

He jerks again, but I…relax. I know how to deal with this

shit, know how to cope with it—*ha*—okay, so I know how to box it up and shove it down and move forward.

"You know I won't give you any money," I remind her.

"I need it for rehab."

Another old page from the playbook, which is why I counter with the same thing I've told her a hundred times, "You know that I'll pay the facility for it directly if you go."

A long pause, the cacophony of noise seeming to rise up and take over.

"I need it for food."

"You know I'll send a grocery delivery to your apartment."

"I don't live there anymore."

Of course not.

"You know I'll arrange for you to pick up some food nearby wherever you are. What do you feel like?"

Another pause.

And then I feel the mood shift, that tautness in the air that any kid from an abusive household feels—the razor's edge of anger, having crossed the point of no return.

"Just wire me the money, you fucking selfish bitch!" she snaps and I feel Cam jerk next to me.

Guilt churns—he hasn't seen this side of a mother, and I know I'm fucked up for exposing him to it.

But…

His hand stays where it is.

And some deep seated wound in my heart begins to knit itself closed.

I inhale, exhale. "You know that I won't," I tell her evenly. "Same as you know that you won't change my mind, no matter how much you yell."

Cam's fingers tense.

"Now," I go on, "would you like me to order you takeout from somewhere?"

"Always a useless selfish pain in my ass," she shouts. "What would it take for you to send me a hundred bucks? Nothing!"

I close my eyes. "Everything," I say quietly.

"Your father would be so disappointed in you."

I open them again. "He made his disappointment clear while he was alive."

Cam's grip tightens then loosens, as though he's worried he'll hurt me.

As though he's worried I could feel anything except for icy cold right now.

"So, you aren't going to send me my money?"

"Goodbye, Mom," I say by way of answer. "I wish you well. If you change your mind about rehab or the food, please let me know."

"Athena Phillips"—there's desperation in her voice now—"don't you fucking dare hang up on—"

I hit the button and disconnect the call.

The silence that's left behind in its wake is terrible.

Then Cam curses quietly and gets up.

My heart sinks as I stare down at my phone, watching her call back, listening to it buzz.

I showed him.

I made him see.

And now he's going to leave.

The call cuts off.

Starts up again.

I reach for my phone but a big hand takes it from me, rejects the call and turns the whole thing off.

I blink.

Look up to see that he hasn't left.

That he's here—right next to me.

"Come here, cupcake."

Before I can so much as turn my head, Cam's tugging me out of the chair, wrapping me tightly in his arms. One hand sinks into my hair, the other rubs lightly up and down my back.

"I—"

"Shh," he says quietly. "I don't need an explanation."

"She's terrible," I whisper.

"Yes."

That he agrees without preamble does something to me—cracks through the ice, I guess. Though any hope of shielding myself from him has already splintered and melted into nothing these last few days.

There are so many reasons for me to keep my distance—not the least of which includes that fucked-up phone call—but...

I can't seem to locate any.

Reasons and self-control and distance.

Not with him hugging me tightly.

The words just...

Keep flowing.

"My dad wasn't any better," I admit.

"That doesn't mean that you're a bad person."

"You knew my upbringing was troubled," I say. "But it's one thing to know and another to experience."

"And yet," he says again, "That doesn't mean you're a bad person."

I exhale, want to shake my head and disagree, just on principle, but with his arms around me, I'm able to...

I don't know, just sit in the moment.

Think that maybe...he's right.

"Enough, cupcake," he says gently. "Don't waste your energy coming up with an excuse to fight that fact." He strokes a hand up and down my back, holding me tightly against his hard chest. "Just let me hold you."

So...

I do.

For long moments, I sit in this fantasy and let him hold me.

And pretend my mom isn't my mom, that my dad wasn't my dad.

And that I'm good.

That I'm not damaged and frozen over and destined to fuck up every wonderful thing in my life.

I just…let him hold me.

Eventually, though, I start getting antsy and slip out of his embrace. "I could use some whisky."

His mouth twitches, but his eyes tell me that he knows precisely what he thinks of my avoidance—it's bullshit.

"Kudos on letting me hold you for"—a glance at his watch—"four minutes and twenty-two seconds." A beat. "And we're out of whisky."

I scowl.

"Damn," I mutter.

"But we *do* have more—" His arms tighten around me, and he doesn't let me escape as he walks us backward and reaches for—

I hear a crinkle.

"—gummy worms."

I still.

He leans back enough to meet my eyes while holding up the bag. "Want to get your frustrations out on these tiny, innocent faces?"

My heart thuds *hard.*

Because he noticed that?

Then my pulse settles, my panic fades.

Because…of course he had.

CHAPTER TWENTY-ONE

Cam

"I'm surprised you managed to peel yourself away from your sex cabin," King says, saucering a puck in my direction.

I catch it on the blade of my stick, spin, and fire a shot on net.

It flies into the top corner with ease.

Kind of like these last few days have been.

Wednesday afternoon Dan sprung us from river jail—which in actuality, was him cock-blocking me. Yes, he was helping as planned. Yes, I was grumpy about it. No more excuses to stay entwined in each other, to stay naked, to eat and fuck and play video games.

Not that Athena didn't work.

She spent time on the phone, on her laptop, working on her case. Just like I spent time working out—and not just by fucking her.

But now we're back in the Bay, back to reality, back to—

Another puck flies toward me, but I'm not quick enough. It smacks me hard in the stomach.

"Ow," I groan.

King smirks. "That'll learn ya."

"Asshole," I mutter.

He flicks another puck at me, but this time I'm paying attention. "Maybe," he says. "But at least I can catch a pass."

"Remind me to never tell you anything about my personal life again," I mutter.

"Hey," King says, "if I was trapped with a woman in a love shack, fucking her brains out, I'd be shouting it from the rooftops too."

Shouting, apparently, being sending a text to our group chain saying I was busy with a woman and couldn't meet up for kitten time.

I'm still not certain how they got that even much out of me—

But the truth is that I'd caved like a cheap suitcase.

Must be that older brother sniffing out secrets super power.

Or maybe the fact that I'm fucking *happy* and my tongue was loosened.

I send the puck back to him—hard, much harder than we've been passing. Mostly because today is just about getting some ice time and fucking around, staying loose, finding the joy in the sport again. Not trying to kill each other, even though I'm not opposed to giving my annoying teammates a couple of bruises. Unfortunately, for me King just catches it without issue, sending it sailing over to Rome, who takes a shot.

Ping!

There's nothing like that sound, especially when it's resulting in a bar down—the puck bouncing into the net instead of hitting a post and bouncing out.

Hudson, who's standing next to me, whistles. "Goddamn, the man's got a shot."

I look over at my teammate—or maybe I should say that I look *up*.

He's a big fucker, one of the biggest on the roster and built like a tank. But contrary to most of the absolute units in the league, Huddy is fast as hell, liquid lightning. And it doesn't take half a sheet of ice for him to get going.

He's got great hands too.

And isn't a douchebag.

So, we've looped him into our whole *not* asshole group.

"You say that as though you didn't break someone's hand with *your* clapper."

Huddy's a modest guy, and he doesn't have to be.

But, as is his way, he just shrugs and turns the focus to someone else, in this case, complimenting Rome. "Cap's accuracy is unmatched." One big shoulder lifts and drops. "If I had a modicum of that…"

See?

Modest.

And smart. Fucker takes college classes for fun.

"Modicum's a big word, Huddy."

He just shakes his head, picks up a puck, and gets down to business. But I see that he's smiling.

Grinning, I scoop up my own puck, get some time in on the ice. It's a rare commodity in the summer time, and it feels like home just being on the rink. Cold air, crunching skates, the slaps and pings and crashes that are hockey personified.

By the time our hour's up, I'm sweating and my wrists and forearms ache. There's nothing that can quite replicate being on the ice…except for *being* on the ice, so it's good to get out here.

Good to get time just doing what I love, what I know, what feels right.

Athena.

Well, that too, I think with a smirk—or that's what I'm *going* to do next.

"Ow!" I grunt, finding my face pressed to the wall outside the locker room.

"Sex cave thoughts," King jokes, easing up on my back so my nose isn't actually plastered against the concrete. "Gotta get your head in the game, kid."

That sends a pulse of guilt through me.

Something he sees.

Fuck.

"Cam," he begins, immediately releasing me.

"What are you and Rory up to today?" I blurt.

"*Cam,*" he says again, his tone filled with warning.

Danger. Danger.

But, thank fuck, Rome comes down the hall then, discussing something in depth with Huddy.

"I need to talk to Rome," I say quickly.

King opens his mouth, but I'm already moving, using one of my patented youngest sibling moves to dodge the arm he shoots out.

"Hey." I'm interrupting, but I don't have a fucking problem with being a rude fucker—not when it means avoiding the conversation with King. God knows, it's bad enough that Athena knows everything—

Bad.

Okay, that's not fair.

It's…fine. She knows about the injury and Coach, but that doesn't mean I want everyone else to know about the bullshit that was fucking with my head.

I'm fine. It'll all be fine.

And I've even talked with someone about it.

See? Growth. Ready to move forward.

But I don't get a chance to have my fake conversation with Rome to avoid King's conversation.

Because Coach comes out of his office.

He gets one glimpse of me, scowls, and bellows, "Jackson. Your ass in my office. *Now.*"

THINGS WERE GOING GOOD.

But now I'm sitting in a familiar chair, listening to a familiar rant, and trying to remember why I'm here, putting in extra time in the off-season, only to get shit on for my "lack of seriousness" on the ice.

Never mind that the guys and I paid for the ice time. Never mind that we were *all* free and loose and this was far from an organized team practice. Never mind that I wasn't the only one pausing to chat and fuck around and laugh and just generally enjoy the thing that's been our lives from pretty much the moment we started walking.

"…fucking hell, Jackson. You need to—"

There's a knock at the door, and I look up just in time to see the door swing open, to see Chrissy pop her head in. There's something in her eyes that I don't love—that I fucking hate, that tells me she heard enough of Coach's rant.

Damn.

"Are we still having that meeting, Barry?" she asks, tone completely neutral but somehow still displaying complete disapproval.

Chrissy doesn't strictly work for the team—her full-time gig is her animal charity—but she does contract work on the player development side, mostly because she's really gifted at it, but also because Jean-Michel likes to play overprotective dad and keep her close so he can protect her.

Or *over*protect as she likes to complain.

But when our eyes connect, I know that the overprotective gene didn't skip a generation.

"I can come back," she says when Coach doesn't immediately reply, starting to turn, her tablet and papers in hand.

That snaps him out of his stupor, and he narrows his eyes for a second before he glares at me again. "Dismissed."

Not liking that look and what it might mean for Chrissy, I flick my eyes toward her as I stand up, wanting to make sure she knows I won't leave her unless she's comfortable.

Her half-smile and the amusement creeping into her expression tells me enough.

Christina Dubois may have a soft heart for stray animals and people, but she's her father's daughter.

And if she needs to kick some ass, that trait didn't skip a generation either.

I nod, slip from the room, and make short work of getting changed and heading out to my parking lot.

But my run-ins with the Dubois doublet doesn't end with Chrissy intervening in Coach's office.

The moment I step out into the California sunshine, I spot someone by my car.

No. *Someones*.

The owner of the team, Jean-Michel Dubois, is talking to…

Athena.

CHAPTER TWENTY-TWO

Athena

I'VE BEEN WAYLAID by a silver fox.

Or, I suppose, *I* did the waylaying.

Jean-Michel Dubois might be a successful businessman who owns vineyards around the world *and* a hockey team—bottles and blades, who would have thought that combination might work?—but I can't deny that there's something that draws my focus to him.

And *only* him.

It's an actual struggle to remember my surroundings, to not get sucked into the black-hole-like pull that is Jean-Michel.

Maybe it's the French Canadian accent.

Maybe it's the strongly built body that doesn't speak of a man in his late forties.

Maybe it's the hint of salt in his dark brown hair.

Or maybe it's that he's ruthless with those who fuck him or his loved ones or his businesses over, but that he funds his daughter's cat charity—and that includes support staff and veterinaries and vet techs along with reimbursing the volunteers who take care of the innocent animals.

Maybe—

Okay, maybe it's *all* of that.

Along with the fact that we investigated him so thoroughly I can tell you exactly how many billions this many is worth—down to the penny—and I didn't find a single illegal act.

Immoral? Maybe.

But I happen to approve of Jean-Michel's brand of justice.

Come after his family—you'll face the consequences.

Come after his businesses—you'll end up bankrupt.

But come at him with innovation and competition and hard work, and he'll invest, compete, or cede that line of business, depending on what's the best use of his time.

Gotta respect the standards.

Especially when he built his empire from the ground up.

No rich daddy seed money here.

"You've been investigating me," he says, eyes fixed on mine as I lean back against Cam's car. It's been a couple of days since I've seen my hot hockey hunk—my fault because I needed time in the office—but even though I framed this foray to my team as necessary so I could make contact with Jean-Michel and warn him that he might need to amp up his private security, in reality, I jumped on the chance to ensure our interaction happened here.

Where Cam is.

"Yes, we *have* been investigating you," I say and have the pleasure of seeing surprise skate across his handsome face.

I don't think he's surprised often.

And that's…well, I decide I get my gold star for the day.

Go me.

"How'd you know?" I ask when he just tucks the shock away and fixes me in place with an intense stare.

I shiver.

This is a man who'd fuck you on a desk so hard that you'd feel him with every step the next day…and then draw you a bubble bath to make that pleasurable discomfort fade.

Hot as hell.

Grumpy as hell.

But I prefer easy smiles and quiet energy.

That sends a blip of alarm pulsing through me, but, just like I've been doing since Mother Nature decided I needed a few days of hot sex and even hotter hockey player, I push it down and focus.

"You think I wouldn't know when someone's poking around in my accounts?" The question is dry, laced with amusement.

I frown.

We're supposed to be untraceable, invisible, silently observing.

That Jean-Michel noticed either tells me that we've fucked up…or more likely, that he's just that good.

I lift a shoulder, allow it to fall in a halfhearted shrug. "Right."

"Why are you here?"

I study him, wonder how much bullshit I can spin while not affecting Cam's position on the team.

Jean-Michel's face tells me not much.

"I can't say."

His face clouds.

So, I hurry to add, "But I *can* say that if I were a certain owner of varied businesses from wine to sports, an owner who's been looked into and cleared of anything to do with an ongoing investigation, I'd make sure that my security detail was beefed up and—"

My gaze trails to the side where a man who's definitely *not* a silver fox—and has none of the allure of one Jean-Michel Dubois—is walking into the arena, briefcase in hand and a severe expression on his face. I watch as he scans a badge at the arena door, yanks it open like he's ready to unleash the fury within him on whoever gets in his way.

Jesus.

That asshole must be a gem to work with.

"—staying on task to protect me *and* the people I care about," I finish, turning back to Jean-Michel.

He tilts his head to the side. "And is that the *only* reason you cornered me at my place of business?"

"One of them," I say with another shrug.

He flicks his eyebrows up in question.

"I chose this place specifically over your other businesses."

Those eyebrows shoot higher.

"Because"—I lean back against Cam's car—"I'm dating one of your players."

If there's another flicker of surprise in the other man's eyes, it's just that—a flicker, there and gone in the next instant. Then his gaze slides to the side, and he says, "Jackson."

Not a question.

"I will neither confirm nor deny," I say silkily.

His lips quirk, just the slightest bit, and I feel that like a brush of fingers between my thighs.

Dangerous man.

The door to the arena slams shut and he swivels at the sound, face implacable, but I don't miss that his eyes are troubled.

"I have a meeting to get to," he says quietly.

I nod. "I won't keep you."

"You'll just keep waiting for one of my hockey players?"

I fight a smile. "I will neither confirm nor—"

"Deny," he says on a sigh. "You know, some might consider you troublesome."

I smother a laugh. "Oh, I think it's more than *some*."

Now he full-on grins. "Yup, definitely troublesome, Athena Phillips."

And now it's my turn for my eyebrows to shoot upward in question as his expression becomes cocky. "I make it my business to know who's investigating me."

"Touché."

I lean back again Cam's car, cross my arms. "We didn't find anything, you know."

"Oh, I know," he says, that cocky silver fox in charge once more for a flash before I see a streak of protectiveness lace itself into his expression. "Cam's a good one. Don't fuck with his head, yeah?"

I inhale sharply, panic like I haven't experienced for days spiraling through my insides.

But, for some reason, my reaction has Jean-Michel's face clearing.

"What?" I manage to whisper.

He claps a hand on my shoulder, squeezes lightly. "You'll do, kid."

"What are you talking about?" I ask, confused now, though panic is still swirling beneath the bewilderment.

He waves a hand at my face, which is clearly showing the tumult of my emotions, even though that's extremely bad form as an FBI agent. "Only someone who cares would have that reaction."

I inhale again. I want to deny it, but we both know it would be a lie. I *do* care about Cam, and it's nowhere near familial.

"Exactly." He nods approvingly. "So, like I said, you'll do, kid." He drops his hand. "Keep caring and we'll be good."

That has me pulling my head out of my ass and focusing on what's important—Cam. "You know," I tell him. "If you really care about Cam and his head, then I'd get your asshole of a coach in line."

Thunder begins to coalesce at the edges of his expression. "What do you mean?"

"I mean exactly what I said," I tell him, anger bubbling now as I remember Cam's demeanor when we talked, his disappointment, the way he'd been sliced to the core by the lack of support when he was already beating himself up. His coach had made everything worse. "I *mean*, that maybe if your coaching staff was interesting in building players up instead of flogging them when they're struggling, the Eagles would have made it further than the first round of the playoffs."

His eyes narrow, and I half expect him to unleash a load of anger on me.

But then he exhales, his face clears, and he nods. "I'll take that under advisement."

"Really?" I ask, genuinely surprised.

"If I've learned anything in my years in business, it's to listen when people are talking." He nods at me. "You're talking, so I'm listening."

"Just like that?"

His mouth quirks. "Just like that."

"Wow."

"I hear that a lot."

"Color me surprised that the grumpy billionaire has a sense of humor beneath all that—" I wave my hand at his expression, and right on cue… "—*scowl*."

He shakes his head. "Why are all the women in my life determined to torture me?"

Now *I* smile. "It's probably just your face."

A roll of his eyes before he turns for the rink.

But then he pauses, glances back at me.

"Hey, Phillips?"

"Yeah?"

He unleashes that silver-fox, stroke-me-between-my-legs smile.

"You're not interested in adopting a cat, are you?"

CHAPTER TWENTY-THREE

Cam

"How did I get here?" Athena asks on a sigh.

I grin. Because *here* is Chrissy's bright and colorful adoption center, full to the brim with adorable kittens and cats, people who've paid a few bucks to entertain (and socialize) the furry menaces, volunteers, and...*us.*

A member of the public who's about to adopt a cat.

Not me.

But Athena.

Because Jean-Michel convinced her visiting the adoption center was a good idea.

Just *visiting.*

I grin. I knew from the moment that I came out of the arena a couple of days ago to find them in close conversation and overheard the team's owner discussing the work that Chrissy does in great detail, that this would be the result.

Athena, on the other hand, seemed to be in denial that this would be the inevitable outcome—

A cat sitting on her lap, purring like crazy, and staring up at her with eyes that mean she's just placed a huge order for pickup at a local pet store (where, funny story, the volunteers might have mentioned that adopters receive a generous discount at).

This was after having filled out and turned in paperwork to take this little fluffball home.

And after making an appointment with Chrissy's vet to get a checkup and make sure the kitten is in the system there so he stays on track for all of his vaccines.

And this was all *after* placing an online order for extra supplies and food and litter, all of which will be automatically shipped every month.

Prepper.

My girl is a prepper.

I love it.

I love *everything* I learn about her.

"Come on," I say lightly. "You knew exactly what you were in for the moment you walked through the door."

Silence.

Then a scowl.

Before her face clears and she strokes a hand down the kitten's back—an orange tabby who has mischief in his eyes… except when he looks at Athena. She purses her lips and exhales. "Fine. I knew. I just hadn't allowed my logical self to recognize that fact." She cuddles the kitten closer, and continues, affecting Jean-Michel's voice, "If you're going to be around the team, you should understand some of the charity work we participate in" —her eyes come to mine and she drops the grumpy French Canadian—"so, this"—a nod at the kitten—"is all *your* fault."

"Maybe," I say.

"Or *maybe* you're a softie with lots of love for innocent creatures, no matter how hard you try to pretend otherwise."

Her face is a study in juxtaposition—fear and joy, pleasure and retreat—but just like she's done since she jumped me at the cabin, she shoves that down and pushes forward.

Fuck, I love her so much.

"And why don't *you* have a pet?"

"I travel too much." And I was scared to get attached too anything or anyone after the news.

She seems to hear both of those statements because her face gentles—

And I fall in love with her even more.

Not the woman I knew from a distance, the one I'd mooned over for years. But rather, the one beneath the icy layers that have melted away. The woman she is in this moment *and* the one she has been in the past. The one who cuddles a kitten and comes to the arena. The one who's simultaneously kicking ass in the shooting range and working on a case against an organized crime conglomerate. The one with baggage but who still manages to be a great friend. The one who offers to pay for food and rehab for her deadbeat of a mother.

The one who hugged me because I looked sad.

And the one who opened up when I talked about what was bothering me, sharing so I wouldn't be vulnerable alone.

I've fallen in deep with Athena—deeper than I ever thought possible.

And I can't seem to stop.

Don't *want* to stop.

"Plus, I intend to be an excellent cat dad." I hold up my phone, showing her what I've just bought—a crocheted super-hero mask that will allow the kitten to battle to save Gotham. "And first step is bribing you with adorable hats for the fluffball."

Her eyes narrow, but I don't miss the amusement in the brown depths as she continues petting and says, "Thor would be a superior superhero for him to represent." A kiss to his head, this woman who kept herself so distant and yet holds that kitten like he's the most precious cargo on the planet.

Like she'd hold a baby.

Bile burns the back of my throat, and I exhale slowly.

More than one way to make a family.

More—

"And his name isn't fluffball." She wrinkles her nose at me. "That's far beneath him."

"True," I agree. Plus, he isn't all that fluffy. His fur is sleeker, the orange—along with his demeanor—more understated than his kitten pals creating chaos through the various rooms of the adoption center. "So, what are you going to name him?"

I already know his moniker isn't going to remain Rex—the name the rescue group gave him, this round of kittens named after dinosaurs.

She sighs, lifting him up to study his face. Nonplussed, the kitten blinks green-brown eyes and yawns widely before lying limply against her shoulder and going back to purring loudly. "I don't know."

I run my fingers through his soft fur, ignoring the way he slits his eyes open and glares. "It'll come to you."

"I hope so."

"It will."

But those words didn't come from my mouth and we both shift to watch Chrissy sink down in front of us, looking bright and beautiful…and pregnant.

I feel another pulse slice through my belly—pain and longing and guilt—but thankfully it's not the *only* thing I feel. Sitting next to Athena, watching her with the kitten, and I'm feeling the same sense of completion that I had up at the cabin, especially when she smiles up at me.

My future shifted, things were taken from me.

But that doesn't mean I can't pivot with it, can't be fucking *happy*.

That's what I need to focus on, need to move toward.

"You okay?" Athena asks and for a second I think she's talking to me.

Then I realize her focus is on Chrissy—who went pale, clamped a hand to her mouth, and then rushed out of the space not five minutes ago.

Yup.

Definitely pregnant.

Chrissy's hand shifts slightly, covering her belly, and she nods. "It's…" Her eyes flick to Athena's. "Well, we're not really telling anyone, and the timing won't be great"—to mine—"in terms of the season, but Rome and I are…" She looks around, drops her voice. "Pregnant."

Another pulse, but that's gone the moment Athena shifts and presses her thigh to mine, offering silent comfort.

Not distant.

Not pulling away.

Coming close. *Mine.*

"Congratulations," she tells Chrissy softly.

"Congrats," I say, proud my voice is even.

Chrissy tilts her head to the side, studying me. "Why don't you sound surprised?"

I wince. "I suspected, considering how closely Rome has been hovering." Even now our captain is in the corner of the room, watching Chrissy intently as he changes out some of the cat perches and climbing apparatuses that are looking a little worse for wear.

He narrows his eyes at me and nods, as though warning me to not upset his woman.

I nod back, silently communicating that I wouldn't dare… and that I owe him a celebratory beer.

A kid.

Jesus, that feels like a big step.

That I'll never have.

I grit my teeth together.

Athena shifts a little closer.

I shove the grief down, *deep* down. This isn't about me, isn't about what I lost. This…is about people I love having things that make their lives complete.

"I'm really happy for you both," I say softly, leaning in to hug her around the kittens and cats who've already moved in to claim her. "You'll be great parents."

Her smile is as bright as her soul. "Thank you," she whispers, hugging me back. "That means a lot coming from you."

I exhale, tug a strand of her hair, then wince as a kitten uses my leg for a scratching post. Scooping it up, I cuddle it close as she keeps talking.

"We wanted to wait to tell everyone until the twelve week mark," she says then makes a face. "Unfortunately, me having to run off and puke every thirty minutes is making that hard."

"The kid has his own time frame already, huh?" Athena teases.

That has Chrissy smiling, and it widens as Rome sits behind her and hugs her close.

"Definitely strong-headed like his mom," she agrees, grinning up at Rome and pressing a kiss to his jaw.

"I can't wait to see what she's like," he murmurs.

"*She* huh?" Chrissy asks and I have the feeling this is a conversation they've had many times already. "How do you know *he's* not a boy?"

"I know, kitten." He leans in and kisses the top of her head. Then he glances up at me, his expression shrewd and filled with curiosity.

I brace, knowing this moment has been coming from the moment I walked in with Athena.

"What's up with you two?"

I shoot him a glare.

Jesus, not even going to softball that question?

"Sex cave," he mouths.

Ugh. Well, I guess compared to *that* line of questioning, I should be happy he went the route of playing dumb.

"This is Ats," I say quietly.

"Yeah, I know," he says, drawing Chrissy closer. "We met. We talked—"

"Ats as in *Athena*."

He stills and I know he gets how big this is.

That's what getting drunk and staying up way too fucking late in a hotel bar will do.

Deepest darkest secrets blurted out with every additional shot.

Most of them, anyway.

"*This* is Athena?"

"Ats," she corrects carefully. "You haven't earned the right to call me by my full name." Her lips quirk. "Plus, I don't relish being confused for your pooch."

Also named Athena—a rescue corgi whose litter was named after Roman and Greek gods and goddesses.

Rome recovers quickly, his eyes dancing at her barb. "Noted…Ats. So, you're the childhood friend?"

"Less childhood and more family," she says bluntly. "I've known Cam for a decade."

Worry in his eyes. "And is that how long you've been in love with his brother?"

"Rome," I snap. "What the fuck?"

Chrissy swats him across the chest at the same time, sending the kittens scattering. "Seriously?"

"It's not any of your business," Athena says quietly. "But I've never been in love with Cam's brother. He's my best friend and that's all he's ever been, all he will ever be."

But Rome doesn't let up. "Because he's with someone else?"

"Dude." I lift the kitten in my lap and set it to the side, ready to drag Rome's ass out of here so I can introduce him to my right fist properly…and in private.

"No," she snaps. "Because Lex and I have been friends forever and never been more." Bald words. "And…"

I find myself holding my breath.

"Because I didn't know Cam had feelings for me."

CHAPTER TWENTY-FOUR

Athena

My heart is pounding, and I'm panicked, desperate to run the fuck out of here.

But my kitten is sleeping, and Cam is tense as a slab of concrete and…

I need him to hear this too.

Because…I'm falling for him.

As dangerous and stupid and likely as that is to blow up in my face. I can't let him go, can't push my feelings down, can't pretend there's nothing between us.

We have something.

I can't cut the ties between us, not even if I wanted to.

"I've known the Jacksons for ten years," I say. "I've known Lex for longer, and they're…well, they're my family, so much more than my own parents ever were. So, if there's ever anyone in my life I wouldn't hurt, wouldn't fuck over, would do *anything* to protect it's the Jacksons—Cam included."

"So, it's brotherly affection then?" Rome asks, and I don't miss that his eyes are sharp.

Waiting for me to fuck up.

I can't.

This is too important.

Cam is too important.

"You know it's not," I say quietly.

"I do?"

I lift a brow. "You *do*." I shift a little closer to Cam, set my hand on his thigh. "But more importantly, *Cam* knows that."

Rome tilts his head to the side and studies me closely.

Then one half of his mouth curves as he raises his fist between us for me to bump. "I like you, Ats."

"Good," I say, reaching forward to tap his knuckles with mine. I smirk at him and am only half-joking when I add, "Me too."

Half because…

I like the person I am with Cam Jackson.

"Meow!"

Cam leans in and scratches my kitten's head. "Relax, Cookie, she hasn't forgotten you," he murmurs, running his knuckles down along the outside of my arm, making me completely aware that he hasn't forgotten me either.

Cupcake.

Cookie.

Yeah, that's perfect.

Cookie stretches in my arms, his whiskers tickling me as he sniffs at my nose. And when his rough tongue laps over the tip, I laugh, gaze sliding to the side—

Breath hitching when I see Cam watching.

"Beautiful," he whispers and my heart thuds hard, feelings rippling through me—too big, too beautiful, too *wonderful.*

"Cam, I—"

"Excuse me!"

I jerk back, not having realized I was leaning in to Cam, having completely forgotten we're in a public place.

With an audience.

One of whom is clamping a hand to her mouth, jumping to her feet, and running away.

Rome gets up and follows her, and I don't miss that Cam watches him go, don't miss the grief he quickly banks.

He'll be an excellent father.

I know it.

Just like I know that *he* knows family isn't just genetics.

But I can't help him with what he lost, can't make that better—

"Meow!"

My heart rolls over in my chest as I look down at Cookie.

I still.

Or maybe I *can* help him see that.

With Cat Dad duties.

———

HE TIPTOES down the hall and into my kitchen, smile wide, but expression tired. "He's finally asleep."

I grin and set the plate down in the sink, the warm water running over my hands, sweeping suds and food remnants down the drain..

We're at my house, having eaten a delicious meal that Cam cooked for us, and, as predicted, Cookie has us both wrapped around his adorable tiny toe beans.

On Chrissy's advice, he doesn't have full reign of the house yet, so we've been taking turns "putting him to bed"—or really, containing him in my bathroom until he's a little more comfortable with where the litter box and water bowl and other cat accoutrements are.

"I told you I'd get the dishes," he says, coming over to the sink, wrapping his arms around my middle, and pressing a kiss to my nape.

"And I told you *I'd* get them," I reply tartly.

He nips at the shell of my ear. "Stubborn."

"Jackson meet Phillips."

He chuckles as I finish up with the last dish, setting it in the drying rack and turning to face him.

"Your version of pot meet kettle?"

"Does it not fit?" I ask archly.

"Of course it does." He pressed a kiss to my forehead. "But I still would have done the dishes, cupcake."

"I know you would have." I turn back to the counter, reach for a towel. "Which is why *I* did them."

Silence...then a swat to my ass.

I squeak.

"And now you're going to pay the price for your insolence."

"With orgasms?" I ask eagerly, glancing over my shoulder.

He narrows his eyes, but humor is dancing in the hazel depths. "I'm not sure you deserve them now."

Them.

Mischief wells up in my belly and even though my fingers are on the towel, I let it go...

And grab the nozzle to the faucet instead.

One flick with my other hand has the water on full blast. One pull has the nozzle free, the stream spraying over my hands.

And one...*spin* has that water shooting in Cam's direction.

It splatters against his chest—and ho, mama—the effect that has on the skintight white fabric of his tee nearly sends me to my knees. I resist the urge, not wanting to miss a moment, especially when it's turning see-through, when the water is spreading down his abdomen, along the waistband of his sweats.

Oh sweet baby Jesus, that's even better.

Plastering the material against his groin, outlining the rigid edge of his erection, sticking the material to his strong thighs—

"What the fuck, cupcake?" he asks, and I manage to tear my gaze away from his face, from the shock in his expression. He grabs the nozzle and starts to reach past me, but I don't let him have it. In fact, I point it back at him, get another glimpse of slick, skintight fabric.

His mouth drops open. "What the hell are you doing?"

I grin, sweep my free hand over his stomach.

Now *that's* a sight.

He cups a hand under my chin, tilts my face up. "What the fuck?"

Instead of answering, I point it in his direction again—

And I see the moment he processes the chaos I've created, that I've embraced, that I'm enjoying—

Or rather I *feel* it.

He rips the nozzle out of my grip…

And points it in *my* direction.

Warm water splatters across my chest, and I gasp in surprise. I shouldn't be taken aback. I created this. I *want* this, but the sudden sensation of warm liquid and taut fabric and—

"Oh God," I moan slipping slightly as I lean back against the counter, gripping the edge tightly as Cam bends and takes one of my nipples in his mouth, the heat and wet and layers of fabric the most acute of sensations.

He sucks as he allows the water to pour down my torso, soaking into my tank top, into my pajama bottoms, my underwear.

He groans and suddenly I'm on the counter next to the sink—water and a hard body on my front, the soft damp material of the towel and a counter that's slick enough for our bodies to slide together, that he has to clamp an arm around me so I don't fall beneath me.

Heat and cool. Hard and soft. Fingers and lips and—

My pants are yanked down.

That hot water is directed between my legs.

"Cam!" I cry.

"Oh no, cupcake," he murmurs, nipping at the underside of my jaw, "you started this war…"

I gasp as his fingers join in with the spray of water.

"…and now you're going to finish."

CHAPTER TWENTY-FIVE

Cam

"Finish it?" she asks, head dropping back, eyes half-mast.

"Hmm?" I rip her sodden tank over her head, send it flying across the room.

The rug beneath my feet is soaked, and I shift her so I can direct the stream of water into the sink—well, on her clit and *then* into the sink.

"I'll finish—" I slip a finger into that tight cunt, and she gasps before she finishes, "Th-the war?"

Ah.

"No, cupcake," I say gruffly, stripping her pants off her ankles and tossing them in the direction of her tank. "You'll finish on my fingers"—I slip another inside, already feeling the walls of her pussy clenching around me—"and then on my tongue"—I suckle at her breasts, revel in her moans—"and then on my cock."

A sharp inhale, that cunt convulsing as her orgasm rolls through her.

I fuck her with my fingers, in and out, in and out, prolonging her pleasure with the stream of water, waiting until she's limp and sated before I turn off the faucet, drop the nozzle in the sink and then lift her from the counter.

Onto the wet rug, the soaked material making her eyes flash wide.

I take advantage of that and shove her thighs wide, dropping to my knees and diving for her pussy.

Sweet and tart, slick pleasure on my tongue and tight fingers in my hair. Her hips buck and she grinds against me, seeking out what I'm determined to give her. She's beautiful in her need, determined in her movements, gorgeous as she climbs that peak.

Up. Up. Up. *Over*—

"Cam!" she cries.

A gush of liquid on my tongue, her fingers tightening in my hair, a moan that's so loud, I'd worry it might wake the neighbors if I gave a fuck.

I don't.

Because I'm reaching for my wallet, for a condom.

Rolling it down, barely able to take a breath and make sure she's with me before I thrust home and rut into her like an animal.

"Now," she orders, gripping my hips, her nails biting into my ass.

I notch my cock at her entrance and thrust to the hilt, loving the clamp of her pussy, how she wraps her legs around me as I fuck her hard and fast.

It's hard to gain purchase with so much water on the floor, but I'm determined, and so is she…

And it wouldn't matter if the world was collapsing around us—

I'm making her come again.

Because my own orgasm is right there.

Because I'm not falling without her.

Because I need to feel her clamping around my cock.

Because—

"Cam!" she cries.

I feel it then—the beginnings of her coming apart—and I let go, fucking her hard and fast and across the slick floor, both of us racing for completion, knowing that it's *right there.*

And then it explodes around me, her slick cunt gripping my cock, sparks shooting behind my eyes, pleasure a wave of flames through my body, incinerating me, leaving me a pile of ashes.

Until she picks them up and transforms me into something else.

Something better.

Something *more.*

"I love you," I whisper.

Her body goes still and hope ricochets through my insides.

"Cam," she murmurs, wrapping her arms around me, holding me tight. "You're so precious to me."

Disappointment wars with hope—not the words I wanted, but she's also keeping me close.

Not at a distance.

Not behind ice.

Warm arms around me and a soft body beneath me.

That's enough.

For now, it's more than enough.

Especially when I hear the pitter-patter of little feet and—

"Meow!"

Apparently, Cookie is done being locked up in the bathroom.

THE NEXT DAY, after running far too many loads of towels through the wash, I head to the weight room at the practice facility.

I could go to the gym, but Hudson's working out here this morning and it's always nice to have someone to make sure you don't drop the barbell on your head.

Plus, talking makes the awfulness of the squats my trainer's assigned pass all that much faster.

Huddy's inside, headphones around his neck, big body threatening to split the tight tee he's sporting. He nods once, his usual taciturn acknowledgement, but at least he gives me a commiserating look when we glance over our respective exercise plans.

Shared pain is productive pain.

But the couple of groans and scowls are the only delay we allow ourselves before getting down to business.

"What's this I hear about a girl and a sex cave?" he asks long minutes later, using his quota of words for the day to be nosy as he swipes a towel over his face, his breath coming in rapid gusts.

I groan inwardly.

Gossiping old crones.

Rome and King and now Huddy.

"No sex cave."

"But yes to a girl?"

I sigh, but then I accept the inevitable. Hiding will only make the gossip worse and he's been around King, Rome, and me enough to have *heard* enough. Might as well get it out there and get it over with. "Not a girl," I say. "A sexy, smart woman—"

"You're not talking for *you*, right?" Pat sneers as he strolls into the room.

I roll my eyes, but it's Huddy who steps to my side and glares at Pat.

"What?" Pat asks. "You got a problem, big boy?"

Huddy just narrows his eyes…and picks up an obscenely large dumbbell, starts curling it.

I can't be the only one who's imagining that's Pat's dismembered head, right?

His ego is big enough that it would be a workout and a half just to heft it.

Rolling my eyes, I ignore Pat and hurry through the last couple of exercises. I'm having a great day. I'm not going to let this asshole ruin it.

But when I hitch my chin in Huddy's direction, silently

telling him I'll catch up with him later, and then head for the showers, I realize that a different asshole's going to ruin it instead.

Coach is standing in the hall.

Scowling at me.

"Jackson," he snaps. "My office."

I hesitate for a moment. It's the fucking off-season. I don't owe this man my time. I don't have to listen to his bullshit.

I feel that so strongly, I almost turn to go.

But then he snaps out my name again and my feet start moving and I...

Walk into his office.

And spend thirty minutes listening to a soliloquy on how terrible I am.

At everything from hockey to life.

When he finally dismisses me, the words are buzzing around my brain and my emotions are shoved deep, deep down, and I just want to shower and go home.

Want to see Athena and Cookie and forget that while I've fixed one part of my life, the other huge piece is in disarray.

"Shut the door!" Coach snaps.

I pull the metal panel closed, start walking, but almost immediately skid to a stop when I see Jean-Michel is propping up the opposite wall. His frown has my stomach knotting, even though his tone is completely neutral. "You good?" he asks after a long moment.

I slap a smile on my face, start walking. "I'm great," I lie as I move past him.

"Cam."

"*Really* great," I tell him. "I'm on my way to meet up with Athena and the kitten you conned her into adopting."

None of that is strictly a lie.

But it's not strictly the truth either.

Still, it has him pausing in the hall for a long moment before he nods at me. "Then I won't keep you, but I'll talk to you later, yeah?"

"Of course," I lie before I'm hustling down the corridor, pushing out into the sunshine that's dappling the pavement of the parking lot, hurrying to my car, and getting the fuck out of there.

Which means I never do get my shower.

But I never *do* get everything, do I?

CHAPTER TWENTY-SIX

Athena

I FROWN as I stare at my phone screen, wondering if I'm overreacting but not confident enough in my navigation dating norms to know for certain.

The text from Cam is normal…

And yet, it's somehow completely off at the same time.

Sighing, I rub my forehead, snag my stuff from my desk and decide…fuck it.

If he's fine, I'll apologize.

If he's not, I'll have acted instead of spinning in circles, staring at my computer screen, worrying and unable to focus on the new leads that have come through. Leads that I haven't been able to make sense.

The pieces are here, I know it.

But I can't put them together.

Ugh.

It'll come. I know that, know I can't rush this. But sometimes I wish my job leaned more toward the TV version of being an FBI agent—clicking away on my keyboard for a couple of minutes, shaking down some baddies on the street to find the other bad guys, or better yet, the bad guys revealing themselves, tying up the case in a neat little bow, thus allowing us to move onto the next case, all in less than an hour.

Unfortunately, real life isn't that easy.

But I'll figure it out. I'll crack this.

For Tommy.

For me.

It may take more time than I want, but I *always* get there.

Tonight, though, Cam's more important.

As I'm coming out of my office, bag slung over my shoulders, I see Sandra coming toward me.

My boss's expression is determined, but the moment she sees me packed up, her expression clears. "You're leaving before six?"

A blip of guilt slides through me. "I can stay if you need me to," I say quickly.

Her mouth hitches up. "Ats, seriously?"

"What?" I ask.

"I've been in here, kicking your ass out, telling you to go home practically every day since you joined the team and *today's* the day you think I'm going to ask you to stay?"

"Well"—I shift my backpack—"the criminals don't care if I've worked eight hours."

"Ten," she corrects.

"What?"

"Connie says you've been here ten hours. Which"—a shrug—"I'll give you, it's less than your typical twelve, but get the hell out of here, kid. Go enjoy the fact that it's still light out. This job doesn't always stay at the office, and it gets in the way of sleep and meals and birthdays and—" She smiles. "It likes to pick the moment you most don't want to activate to force you to work. So, get out of here, and if you need me to make that an order so you don't feel guilty, I'm *ordering* you to get a life."

"I'll have you know that my life has been *very* lifey of late."

"Oh?"

"I adopted a cat—"

She smirks. "So it can eat your face when you die and knock over water glasses just to be an asshole?"

My lips quirk, thinking I have a much-preferred method to waste water…and that my kitchen rug will likely never recover. "Well, that, and using the litter box the moment I clean it. Oh, and getting hair on all my"—I swipe at my pants—"clothes."

"Impressive."

"Well," I say lightly. "If you want impressive, you should see my boyfriend."

The words are a throwaway…kind of.

But the way they make me feel—

Damn, I'm in deep. Really fucking *deep.*

And…

I can't bring myself to care.

Sandra's eyes dance. "A cat *and* a boyfriend, consider me suitably chastised about you not having a life."

"Rude."

She grins. "Off with you, kid. Enjoy that life because you know the call to close all this shit down will come sooner rather than later."

———

THERE'S a large black SUV parked in front of my house when I pull into the driveway and I've barely popped my door before Jean-Michel is getting out of the back seat.

A billionaire hanging at my curb, yeah make *that* make sense.

"JM," I say, moving toward him and extending a hand.

He shakes it as he asks archly, "JM?"

I shrug. "Your name's a mouthful," I say, just to see what he'll do. "JM's easier."

I swear his eye twitches.

"Chrissy says you've adopted Rex?" he asks instead of acknowledging that.

"Chrissy is short for Christina, just FYI." A beat. "And yes, I adopted Rex, but he goes by Cookie now."

"Hmm." He nods his head toward the house. "So, am I going to get to see Cookie?"

Clearly, he's not here for the cat, and *clearly* he doesn't want to have this conversation on my front lawn.

"Sure," I say, turning for the front door. "But RIP to those clean black slacks."

He glances down then lifts a brow.

"Cook likes to cuddle," I explain as I unlock the handle and step inside, not missing that one of Jean-Michel's security guards has followed us. "Want to do a sweep?" I ask him.

"Andre can wait there," JM answers, nodding at the other man. "I trust that you're not going to kidnap me and blackmail my estate considering you gave me the warning in the first place."

"And now you've figured out my evil plan to take over the world, muahaha."

He shoots me a droll look but follows me into the kitchen.

"Meow!"

I smile down at Cookie, who's eschewed all notion of being cooped up in the bathroom. "Hey, bud," I say, scooping him up like a baby and scratching his belly—his favorite. He arches and starts purring then seems to finally deign to notice Jean-Michel.

"Meow?"

He jumps out of my arms and darts across the counter, sniffing at the hand that Jean-Michel holds out.

Then butting his head against it and allowing Jean-Michel to scratch him.

No surprise that animals like him, considering all he's done with Chrissy's charity, but having it on display right in front of me confirms what the data has shown.

Jean-Michel is a good guy.

"So, why are you really here?" I ask.

He stills with his fingers sunk into Cookie's fur. "I've emailed you a link to some files."

"When?"

"Five minutes ago."

Lifting my eyebrows, I slip my phone from my pocket and open the mail app, seeing that, indeed, there's an email from Jean-Michel. "What is it?"

"You'll see," he says quietly, running his fingers through Cookie's fur. "Give me something, Ats. Something that I can use to get rid of the asshole. If not for me, then for Cam."

I was already pulling my laptop from my backpack and logging in, but his words have me moving a little faster, clicking the link and—

My gaze shoots up. "You're giving me access to *this?*"

All of the player and staff records from the team, along with emails and flight records and…personal messages.

What the actual fuck?

"I've been trying to figure it out," he says by way of explanation. "Something's off, but there's nothing I can use to break the contract. If we have to fire him and pay out, we have to pay out. But…there's something here I can't put my finger on. Something that tells me there's more going on and firing my head coach won't solve it."

"This have something to do with your ex?"

Scuttlebutt says that his ex-wife recently reappeared in his and Chrissy's lives and is determined to create chaos—

By saying their divorce isn't valid and wanting to come after half of his assets.

All of his assets.

A shrug. "I'm not sure. But if it's fucking up my life, that's more than likely."

I wince. "You know I can't help you with a civil case."

He waves a hand. "I know," he says. "I can handle my ex and the shit storm she's made my life." His expression goes serious. "I'm more concerned because all of Peter's focus seems to be on

Cam. I admit I wasn't as engaged as I should have been at the end of the season and thought we just ran out of steam. But Rome has said a few things and then you mentioned—"

I nod.

"And so…I've been paying attention. We're not even truly back and Cam's already busting his ass in the weight room and today—"

"What happened today?" I ask, head spinning.

I *knew* that text was off.

Thank God I'm home already.

"I heard him screaming at Cam, fucking *screaming*." He shakes his head. "I get that it's sports, that we all want to win—hell, I've made it my fucking *mission*. But"—he sighs—"that's not how I do things in my businesses, and I've made it clear that's not how I want the Eagles handled either. Cam, especially, doesn't respond to someone being on his ass like that. He pushes himself hard enough as it is and someone accusing him of not pulling his weight and it…well…"

"It gets in his head," I finish.

"Yes," he agrees quietly.

Okay. That fucking coach is dead.

Or at least bankrupt, his entire life in shambles.

Or…fired.

Or all three because why the fuck not?

That has me tamping down my rage and focusing. That asshole of a coach is hurting my Cam.

No more.

Lifting my chin, I lock eyes with Jean-Michel.

"I've got this."

His mouth tips up at the edges.

"Oh, I have no doubt of that."

CHAPTER TWENTY-SEVEN

Cam

"Cam."

I blink and look up from the television screen.

"Cupcake," I say quickly, setting my controller to the side and jumping up to my feet at the sight of Athena in my house after I told her I couldn't meet tonight. Worry has my stomach churning. "Is everything okay?"

She shifts, and sets a cat carrier down, Cookie giving a meow in protest. "I think you're the one who owes me that explanation." She moves over and pops me on the chest. "What the fuck, honey?"

The endearment strokes gentle fingers over my heart before the rest of the words process and grip tightly around the vulnerable organ.

"What do you mean?" I ask carefully.

She glares, pulls her phone out, and reads, *"I'm too tired to meet up today?* Really?"

I smother a wince and avoid the question by bending over and unzipping Cookie's carrier. He pops his head out immediately and shoves his face in my hand, demanding that I pet him.

"It's not anything to do with you," I say quietly. "I had a rough day at the gym and—"

"And you didn't think that's something I should know?" she snaps. "Something I could help you with?"

"I—"

"We're in a relationship Cameron Jackson," she continues, the words clipped out. "You said that's you're in love with me. Or has that changed?"

"I—"

"And you've gone and made me fall in love with you too!"

I freeze, hope a blistering wave through my veins. "What?"

She stills, her mouth dropping open. I watch as she takes a step back, another, before I snap out of it and burst into motion.

I'm across the room in a flash, so fast that Cookie hisses and swats at my ankles. I just ignore him, moving to Athena and wrapping my fingers around her wrist, holding her in place when she would have taken another pace back.

"What did you say?" I ask quietly.

She shakes her head. "I'm here for you. Here because I'm worried for you and you pushed me away. What happened?"

"Coach pulled me into his office and was an asshole." I shift my grip, cupping both of her shoulders and turning her to face me completely. "It got in my head, and I needed a couple of hours to decompress."

Her chin comes up. "And you didn't think to tell me?"

I slide my hands down, holding her waist, drawing her close, near enough to feel all of the soft of her against all of the hard of me. "Fair point, cupcake." I touch my nose to hers. "I should have told you." I press a brief kiss to that lush mouth. "Now," I murmur as I pull back, "what did you say?"

Her chest is rising and falling in rapid gusts and for a moment, I think she's not going to answer me.

But then exhales, drops her forehead against my shoulder, and says, "Why is this so fucking scary?"

"Because it's new. Because you were taught not to trust love.

Because I've spent a decade in love with you and I'm long beyond the fear. I just..."

Her head lifts, eyes blazing with emotion as she holds my gaze.

"I just *love* you, cupcake. Every part of you I know and the secrets I'm still unearthing. You're...home. I'm never more settled or quiet or at peace as I am when I'm with you."

"Cam," she whispers.

"I love your strength and beauty and the fact that this is a big step. I love that you've let me in and that you're here, that you knew something was wrong so you tracked my stubborn ass down and forced me to talk. I love that you adopted Cookie and now you've been sending me Reels about cat harnesses and tiny cat doors and adorable hats he can wear."

"You started it," she whispers.

My heart squeezes. "I spent ten years loving a fantasy, baby, only to realize that you're more than I could ever dream up."

"Cam," she whispers, eyes going damp.

"And I love—"

Her fingers press to my lips. "Honey."

There my heart goes again.

"Yeah?" I mumble against her fingers.

"I love *you*." Her eyes slide closed for a beat. Then open and I find that my lungs don't want to work, that my heart has rolled over and offered itself up on a platter. "It's scary and terrifying and I'm half-convinced I'm still going to do something to fuck it up—"

"Cupcake—"

"But...I know you, Cam Jackson. I've spent these ten years learning you, trusting you, understanding you, even if I didn't fully see you for the man you are."

"Athena—"

"I'm sorry for that," she murmurs. "I wish I'd—" A shake of her head. "I wish I'd been open to something sooner. Maybe then you wouldn't have—" She sighs. "Maybe then you wouldn't have had to shoulder everything alone."

"I wish *I'd* said something sooner." I tug at a curl. "Like maybe five years ago." I smile at her. "Because maybe then I would have realized you weren't in love with Lex."

"I wouldn't have been open to anything anyway."

"Why?"

"I—" A sigh. "It wasn't a simple thing. I wasn't open to connection—God, you know how long it took for your parents to win me over, and if I hadn't seen your brothers' relationships, hadn't watched Lex fall, I wouldn't have started to open my eyes and realize what I was missing. I was already feeling…unsettled in my life when we lost Tommy and—" Her throat works. "The move confirmed it. I wasn't dealing with my mom showing up all the time, demanding money, any longer. But I also wasn't in the Jackson fold and…I guess my life was empty. Work isn't the same without Lex, and without that connection, without a boss to let me use it as a safety blanket—because Sandra is determined to help me find work-life balance—I've realized…I don't want to be the person who's entire existence is showing up at the office or solving a case or hiding behind solving everyone else's problems so I don't have to deal with my own bullshit."

"Baby," I murmur, drawing her closer. "How'd you get so smart?"

"Cinnamon rolls."

Surprised, I laugh.

"I'm serious," she says lightly. "If your mom's cinnamon rolls hadn't won me over, I would have still been stuck flailing around in emotional no man's land."

"And now you're in love with me."

She grins. "I am."

"See?" I tease. "That's not so scary to admit."

"Very funny." A swat against my chest, but I capture her hand, press a kiss to her palm.

"You know what this means, right?"

"Know what *what* means?"

I waggle my eyebrows. "We get to have sex."

Laughter bubbles up in her chest. "Don't we do that all the time, anyway?"

"True," I say as I heft her over my shoulder. "But now we get to have celebratory I-love-you sex and that's a hundred times better."

"Considering how—" She grunts as I start taking the stairs two at a time. "Considering how good normal sex is, that's quite a statement to prove."

I drop her on the bed, come down over the top of her.

"Luckily, I'm a hard worker."

She grins. "A *hard* worker," she quips making me chuckle before her face goes serious. "Cam?"

"Yeah, cupcake?"

"Promise me."

I brush my knuckles down the slender column of her throat. "Promise you what?"

"Promise me you won't push me away like you did today. If you need space, fine, but will you please just ask for it next time?"

Damn.

Guilt slides through me as I settle my forehead against hers. "I'm sorry."

"I don't need an apology."

"But I need to give you one." I straighten, cup her jaw. "And I promise to talk to you instead of shutting you out from here on."

She shudders, relief clinging to her expression. Then she nods. "Thank you, honey."

"Any time."

Her smile returns quick and easy, the serious moment replaced with humor and contentment and *home* as she settles back on my pillows, spreads her arms and legs and declares, "I'm ready for the hundred-times-better-I-love-you sex now."

And, thankfully, I'm more than ready to give it to her.
So, I do.

CHAPTER TWENTY-EIGHT

Athena

Cam talked a big game.

And he more than lived up to it.

I'm still sore as hell the following week as I walk into my office, climb the stairs slowly, and come out of the stairwell to Connie's knowing look.

Namely because I've spent every day for the last week hobbling into the bureau because *Cam* has spent our evenings making sure I know precisely how special my love for him is.

I've been wined and dined and orgasmed into submission, and I can't give a fuck.

Because I've been thoroughly *fucked.*

Heh.

"Am I going to meet this boyfriend of yours?" she asks, passing me my now daily and much-needed cup of coffee.

I yawn as I take a huge gulp from the mug, feeling that sweet, sweet blast of caffeine hitting my veins. "No," I say then add when she looks crestfallen, "Okay, *maybe.*"

Her face lights up, and I know I've gotten played as she peels off at my office, waving and saying, "I'll hold you to that."

Sighing, knowing that her statement is fact, I take another sip of coffee and ignore her smug look as I push inside and settle down at my desk, boot up my computer. I pull up the Lyon case file as I sip the coffee, but even though I refill it a half-dozen times over the next hours, it doesn't give me any clarity, and by the time I've had lunch, I've run through all the new information that came in overnight.

Instead of twiddling my thumbs—or banging my head against my desk in frustration—I switch gears, pop into my work email (and know that Jean-Michel's staff is good to have found it), and pull up the message that he sent me.

And I start going through it. Again.

For the umpteenth time over the last seven days.

A click brings up all of those files.

Another gives me access to the personal records of the staff.

It's an intrusion, I know that, and probably a half-dozen steps beyond what any normal employer would give an investigator, but I also trust JM's instincts. If he says something is up with someone in the organization, I believe him.

And, frankly, I would love to find something to nail that asshole of a coach to the wall.

But just like my other run-throughs, today's doesn't yield anything either, and so by the time I'm done looking for any obvious connections, I'm ready to knock off for the day.

Logging out of my computer, I gather my stuff so I can go home, change, feed the tiny he-cat demon, then meet Cam and the others for Game Night at his place.

Yup. The *others.*

As in, his friends and teammates, who are really freaking nice. And while I already knew I liked Chrissy—because kind, lovely cat lady—I *really* like her now. She's sweet and funny and driven and has a cat named Joan of Freaking Arc, who's as badass as the medieval warrior must have been and tolerates Rome's corgi pup with my namesake.

And she's competitive, which I respect, along with her bestie,

Rory, who's just as nice, and just as cutthroat as they battle their way through board and video games alike, even though neither had apparently played the latter until Cam introduced them to drug that is battling orcs and dragons.

We women bonded over the difficulties of double-jumps even though my indoctrination started earlier, mostly because Lex and the older Jackson brothers spent their share of hours shooting each other on screen or bickering over a teamwork game that required them to cook a meal together.

If I had a penny for every time I heard, *"I need more lettuce! Chop faster!"* I would have a lot of pennies.

But we didn't play *Overcooked* last weekend, and I didn't get yelled at about cutting enough vegetables.

Instead, we played old-fashioned board games and threw down over orcs.

And tonight we're doing it all over again.

Smiling, I hurry through my shower, throw on a pair of jeans and a halfway decent shirt then make sure to give Cookie plenty of cuddles and, well, *cookies*. Then I'm out the door, into my car. I buckle in and am halfway out of the garage when the niggle hits—

No, when the *Mack Truck* of a realization hits, slamming into my head with all the finesse of that big truck and leaving me dazed and spinning on the side of the road.

Road.

Shit.

I slam on the brakes, stopping my reverse, and wrench the gear shift into drive. I gun the gas and pull back into the garage with a squeal of tires that's likely loud enough to concern the neighbors.

I'll apologize later, I think, as I slam on the brakes again, stopping mere inches from colliding with the inside wall and slamming the transmission into park.

"Fuck," I whisper as I snag my purse and all but leap out of my car, sprinting for the house. "How did I miss it?"

I tear into the house so quickly that Cookie sprints away from me, knocking over shoes and who the fuck knows what else as he skitters through the house.

"Sorry," I call as I catch the door before it can slam into the wall and close it behind me. But that's all I have time to do as I hurry into the kitchen, pick up my laptop, and open up the Lyon case file.

As I scroll through the files and the notes I made, trying to remember where the fuck I'd seen it.

"Come on," I whisper as I read rapidly. *"Come on."*

My phone buzzes, but I only distantly hear it, and I can't pull my focus from the files anyway.

I need to find it.

Need to put the rest of the pieces together.

I need to…

Find the confirmation of why the asshole of a head coach for the Eagles looked so familiar the other day at the rink.

And as I search for it, I don't hear the texts, don't hear the calls.

I'm just in the zone.

Searching.

Finding.

And by the time the door to the mud room crashes open, who knows how much later, I've printed near-on fifty pages, scribbled my way through almost an entire legal pad, and covered my island with papers.

But…I've figured out the puzzle, sorted out the fucked-up mess of the Eagles, and so I'm smiling as Cam hurries out of the hall and into the kitchen.

CHAPTER TWENTY-NINE

Cam

HER HAIR IS a crazy mess of curls, and her eyes are tired, but she's smiling widely as I rush into the kitchen.

"Cam," she says happily, turning in her chair.

"What the fuck, cupcake?" I snap.

She blinks, her smile fading and though a thread of guilt slides through me, I can't let it go that easily.

"I called at least five times, sent a dozen texts," I grit out, trying to calm my temper, my worry. She's here. She's okay. The house didn't burn down. She didn't get in an accident. She didn't pull up stakes and move back to the East Coast.

"I'm sorry," she says, moving a pile of papers to the side and then another and another, repeating the process until she unearths her phone. She holds it up with a chagrined smile. "I didn't hear it. I was so focused on the fact that the case finally makes sense and—" She lifts her hands, indicating the mess that's taken over her island. "Well, I got the pieces to make sense and...I need to move fast."

"That's great, cupcake." I move toward her and kiss the top

of her head. "I'm sorry I came in like an asshole." I pull back. "But you scared the shit out of me."

She winces. "I didn't mean to." Then her gaze flies to the clock in the microwave. "Shit, I missed all of Game Night, didn't I?"

I nod. "You would have loved it. It was a corgi and kitten fest. Cookie would have fit right in."

"Dang." She wrinkles her nose. "I really am sorry. I just… well, I didn't put the pieces together until Jean-Michel gave me the lead."

I still.

"In fact, we thought he might be in on it at first. All that power. The money. The connections. It would be so easy for him to hide criminal activity—"

My lungs seize.

"I was convinced it *was* him for a time," she says. "But I researched for months, and we cleared him, moved on to other targets, so when he gave me the files—"

"Files?" I croak.

She freezes, guilt sliding across her face. "I know it wasn't right, but he gave me access and I needed to help—"

"With what?"

"The Eagles," she says, nodding at the papers, at the photos of the coaches and many of the back office staff. "And I needed the help with my case—"

"*Your* case?"

More guilt on that beautiful face.

Her case. Tommy. Trying to right a wrong.

No.

Doing *anything* to right a wrong.

And suddenly, it all makes sense—never looking at me twice even after she moved here, not getting involved until things were going wrong with Jean-Michel and the team. I know that work has always been the most important thing in the world to her and more than that, I know this case has bordered on obsession with her.

You're not good enough.

Hurt washes over me.

"Tell me," I say carefully.

"Tell me what?" A hesitant question.

"Tell me that you're only with me because of the case."

Her eyes go wide, but I don't miss the sliver of guilt in the deep brown depths. It has those words—*you're not good enough*—slicing through me again, sinking their claws deep into my heart and tearing it wide open.

"Cam," she whispers. "I can't believe you'd think that." A shake of her head. "It's not— It's not like that at all."

"Don't lie to me," I whisper, head pounding, heart hurting.

"I wouldn't. I love you."

I grind my teeth together.

"And if anything," she says, "being with you, falling for you when you play for someone my team was actively investigating would have made things more complicated between us."

"Gee, thanks," I mutter.

"I don't mean it like that."

She reaches for me but I step back. "Then how do you mean it?"

"I *mean*"—she nibbles at her bottom lip—"that the case doesn't factor into my feelings for you."

I *want* to believe that. I do. I just...

You're not good enough.

"I can't do this right now," I whisper.

She takes another step toward me, hands extended as though to touch me, to hold me. God, I want that, but...

I can't, not when my head is spinning and my heart is sliced to ribbons and nothing makes sense.

I skitter back, hating that the hurt on her face tears through me.

"Cam, honey"—another rip when she halts, when she

doesn't touch me, when that endearment hangs in the air between us—"I didn't even know about your coach until you told me. And I didn't know of his connection to my work until tonight—something that couldn't happen unless Jean-Michel was cleared and felt comfortable enough to give me some files and ask me to investigate."

"When?"

She opens her mouth, closes it. Then opens it again. "When what?"

"*When* did Jean-Michel give you the files?"

"A couple of weeks ago. After we talked that day at the rink. I mentioned to him that your coach was giving you a hard time and—"

Rip!

Jesus Christ.

She'd mentioned my insecure, whiny bullshit to the *owner* of the team.

Who then had swept in to solve all of my problems and recruited my girlfriend to help along the way.

Shame rises up and sweeps over me.

Not good enough. Never going to be good enough.

Can't even deal with my own fucking job.

"I can't do this." The words are torn out of me, but it's what they do to her face that kills me.

And yet, it doesn't stop me from repeating them when she asks, "What?"

"I. Can't. *Do.* This."

A long, horrible silence.

"Can't do what exactly?" she asks quietly.

"This. *Us.* I need some space," I add desperately when her expression locks down, becomes ringed with ice and the fear of losing her overrides the panic in my mind. "You said if I needed space, I could ask for it and you wouldn't hold it against me."

Quiet again, the lack of any words, any sounds other than our breathing just as horrible as the previous silence.

"You're right," she murmurs. "I did say that."

"Well, I need that space now," I say, knowing I sound like a pathetic asshole, but unable to stop as the chant of *You're not good enough* ricochets through my brain.

"Because you think what exactly?" she asks. "That I'm with you because of my case? Even though Jean-Michel and I didn't talk until after what happened between us at the cabin? Until after I'd fallen for you? Until after I realized I love you?"

I want to believe that. *All* of it.

So badly.

But…I can't.

I inhale, my brain shouting at me, but not loudly enough to be heard over that incantation.

You're not good enough. You're not good enough.

"I need to go," I rasp. "I fucking *need* to go."

Silence, long enough this time to slice down to the marrow of my soul.

Then she turns back to her laptop and says quietly, "Then go, Cam."

I hear it in her voice, the resignation, the acceptance, the knowledge that this day would come, and I fucking hate all of that.

But I can't stop myself from spinning away from her.

From striding into the hall, passing Cookie—and the accusations in his gaze—on the way out.

Same as I can't stop myself from driving away, from going home to my empty house, from shutting off my phone and losing myself in a bottle of whisky.

But even that doesn't make the chant go away.

CHAPTER THIRTY

Athena

I PUSH out of the stairwell and step onto the floor to the knowing —and pitying—look on Connie's face.

She passes me a mug of coffee without a word, and I'm grateful that she's given it a rest.

Space.

It's been a *week* of space.

A week without a word from Cam.

I gave in and texted two days ago.

But he didn't respond, and now I'm back to my normal pre-Cam life—pulling twelve-hour days and finalizing a raid on a warehouse in the outskirts of Oakland, its ownership hidden in a long line of shell companies, no tie to the Lyon's evident.

At least until I'd realized exactly who Peter Auclair was—or rather, who he's *related* to.

Second cousin to Frankie's father, Francis Lyon, former head of the Lyon crime conglomerate.

Peter Auclair has all sorts of connections…

And a gambling addiction.

Including on NHL games.

Including on Eagles' games—and most often, betting *against* them.

Fucking asshole.

But he also sold a property in Oakland to a local mid-level crime boss who we know is involved in illegal activity. So now it's putting pieces in place to nail Peter Auclair *and* stake out the warehouse.

The last week of digging has unearthed up several unsavory actors with their fingers in the criminal pie, all with rap sheets a mile long.

Now it's a matter of narrowing them down while keeping an eye on the warehouse *and* shutting down the last outlet of the Lyon's favorite money-making schemes.

Trading in people.

Innocent women. And girls.

That's the worst part. They're trafficking fucking underage girls who have no safe space and get swept up in shit that's dangerous and over their heads, and they have no way to get out—

No more.

It *has* to stop.

And well, gee, I wonder where I got *that* drive to do something—*anything*—good came from.

Because even though Cam *hasn't* called, my mom's been blowing up my phone.

Buzz-buzz.

Ugh. Right on cue.

I rub the throb at my temple, skim through the text that's both a plea and an insult, and then I thank Connie for the coffee and head into my office, doing my best to go about my day. I need to process the intel coming in, need to forward any new leads, and then I have to get out of here early enough to get some sleep.

I was on stakeout duty last night, and though I have tonight off, that doesn't really mean anything.

The pieces are in place, but an earthquake could hit at any time, rattling the parts free, shaking out some rats who'll nibble on the corners. It could easily all blow up and when it settles, still make sense, still mean that the puzzle pieces fit, or it could all explode and send everything we've worked toward scattering toward the four corners of the planet, never to be united again.

We're walking the tightrope of time to gather information and time to fucking act already.

But soon enough we'll be taking that swan dive onto the acting side of the canyon.

And I don't know exactly how soon that will be.

So, I need sleep.

And tomorrow night I'll be back on stakeout duty.

I inhale slowly, exhale just as slowly, and push down my fatigue so I can focus on the intel, can do my necessary research, can get through all of my work and go home to rest—and do that all before I have to endure another one of Connie's pity coffees.

Okay, the coffee's fine.

It's the looks that come with it…and the fact that I must look miserable enough that she hasn't asked when she's going to meet Cam again…

And that the department dinner for spouses and agents she previously scheduled has mysteriously disappeared from our team's joint calendar.

My heart throbs, but like I've done for the last week, I shove down the hurt and focus on work.

Cam needed space.

I gave it to him.

That was the right thing to do.

I just…well, I can't stop thinking that I should have made him stay, should have made him see, made him understand just how much I love him—

Buzz-buzz.

"Ugh," I groan, knowing that, sooner or later, the whole space thing is going to end—whether it's because he comes to his senses or because I run out of patience and end up smacking some of that sense into him, I don't know.

I just...

Can't exist in this limbo any longer.

But...I *can* give him some more time.

Not *much* more. But...*more.*

Buzz-buzz.

Sighing, I flip my phone over, know what I'm going to see on the screen—or some variation of it—even before my eyes trace over the words.

And yup.

My mom wants money.

I type out my normal response, offering food or to pay for a hotel room or to set her up in rehab, but this time, when I go to send it...I hesitate.

Hit the backspace button.

What has she done for me?

Martha's cinnamon rolls and wonderful hugs. Cam's gentle hands and teasing words. Lex's unwavering support. Chrissy's smiles. Rory's shoulder bumps. Cookie nuzzling my face when the tears threatened to come.

They deserve my time, my energy.

My love.

But my mom?

Why do I keep doing this?

Buzz-buzz.

I look...and see more vitriol, more hatred, more...

Not Jackson.

And...I'm tired. Done.

"Enough," I whisper, tapping at that button until I delete the entire reply.

But that's not enough.

Not when it's making me feel like this.

So, I hold my breath as I tap the screen and...block her.

Yes she's my mother. Yes, she provided half of my DNA.

Yes, I have this yearning need to protect people. Full stop.

Even those I don't like. Even those the rest of the world doesn't see the value in.

I *have* to believe that they can change, can be better.

Because otherwise how can I believe that the strides I've made in my own life are long-lasting? How can I believe Cam will see, will understand, will come back to me?

And without that belief, how can I know that I won't turn out like her?

So, I've clung to the ashes of a relationship, desperate to make it make sense, to work, to give me what I need.

For years, I've clung to it.

But…I don't want to any longer.

It can't be what I need.

I want this time and energy to go elsewhere—to go toward building a life with Cam and making friends like Rory and Chrissy, and helping people who aren't trying to constantly use and hurt me.

I need to unload this heavy burden.

I need to be done so I can move forward.

So…

I block her number and delete her texts, and I give myself a sliver of peace before I wrap up my work, head home, and spend the late afternoon napping and cuddling with Cookie.

And hoping that Cam comes back to me.

"Meow!" Cookie chirps hours later, making biscuits on my face until I'm awake enough to give him dinner.

"Fine," I mutter, filling up his bowl and checking his automatic water fountain before heading to the fridge. I should cook something healthy and balanced.

With vegetables.

Instead, I decide on a cinnamon roll, a bag of gummy worms, and two fingers of whisky.

It's a painful reminder of Cam…and also the thing that sends the last of my patience splintering.

"Why the fuck am I standing here miserable and alone?" I mutter, going for my phone. Enough is enough. I'll call him, *make* him listen.

And if he doesn't pick up…

Well, then I'll let myself into his place again and *make* him see reason.

There. *Done.* Good plan. *Break.*

Only, I know that neither of those is going to happen the moment my fingers wrap around my phone.

Call it instinct, but I already know who's calling, even before I flip it over to see the screen.

And…yup. One glimpse of the number there tells me I'm right.

Making Cam see sense tonight is off the table.

Along with that cinnamon roll and the gummy worms and the glass of whisky.

"Phillips," I say after swiping my finger across the screen to answer the call.

"Rendezvous at the warehouse in forty-five," Sandra orders, disconnecting before I can reply.

Sighing, I put the cinnamon roll back in the freezer, dump the whisky down the drain, and then gear up, head out, and—

Set about doing what I'm best at.

Work.

And only work.

But I take the gummy worms with me.

CHAPTER THIRTY-ONE

Cam

I CRACK open my beer and sigh, looking at the paused game on my TV and wondering when in the fuck I've become so pathetic.

I know, of course.

The moment I asked for *space* instead of talked about my feelings.

But it's easier to lament about the fact that I'm a professional hockey player losing himself in video games on a Saturday night than my idiocy.

Easier to berate myself for spending a Saturday morning and afternoon playing video games by myself, followed by that Saturday *night* sharing a pizza with…myself.

After spending a week holed up in my misery, knowing I'm being a whiny toddler and unable to take the steps to fix it.

Unwilling to.

And to make matters worse—or better, depending on which way my mood is swinging—Rome and King have lives, so they haven't been on my ass, digging through the mess that's my head, and though Huddy looked at me sideways yesterday at the gym—probably because I ignored Coach's huffing and puffing and yell-the-house-down presence invading the weight room instead of engaging with it—he's not the type to sit down for a gab fest.

He did invite me to grab a beer with him—which told me enough: I'm looking as pathetic as I feel—but the gym was all I could manage. The idea of sitting in public, making small talk (however limited that would be with the taciturn Huddy) and watching women swoon over him gave me hives.

He'll likely charm them with his mysterious quiet instead of pushing them away, creating drama and a tangled mess that he'll be at a loss to sort.

And I would have sat there, knowing I'm being stupid, knowing I need to call her and apologize, but unable to take that step.

Sighing, I close the box of cold pizza and sit back on the couch with a groan.

So, my in-person friends have well-rounded lives.

And it's late enough that even my online friends aren't around right now to kill orcs and cast spells and generally play the world's nerdiest game.

Yup. I've hit a new low.

Of course, I could just pick up the phone and call Athena.

In fact, I almost do just that…

But it's late.

She needs her rest.

I'll call tomorrow—

And I'll ignore the fact that I've been saying that for a week now as I pick up my controller and dive back into the next quest.

I do it drinking whisky and nibbling on cold pizza crust.

"Yup," I mutter. "I. Am. Pathetic."

I jab at the buttons, recharge my mana, upgrade my spells, collect some gold and several orc skins, and I'm just returning to town to turn in my loot when there's a knock at the door.

I toss the controller to the side in a hurry, far too excited by the prospect of someone saving me from my pathetic night to care who's on the other side—

Hoping it's Athena so I can apologize.

Or if not, maybe it's King and Rory, and Rome and Chrissy with their pups, invading for an impromptu insanely late game night, making me forget that I haven't cuddled Cookie in a week.

Hell, maybe it's a fucking door-to-door salesperson and I can make awkward small talk while being sold an overpriced carpet cleaner at midnight.

I don't even care.

Anything's got to be better than sitting here, muttering about my mana levels and searching an animated forest for random chests of gold.

I push up from the couch, move to the front door, pull it open, and—

My heart leaps.

I freeze. "Cupcake?"

Her mouth opens, but before she can yell at me for being an idiot, for making her make the first move to fix us, for putting us both through the shit when she was doing something to help me, she wavers, her hand going to her side, and—

"Cam," she rasps, her knees giving way.

"*Fuck!*" I lurch forward, grabbing her before she collapses to the hard concrete of my porch.

She cries out when I catch her, when I lift her up and hold her against my chest, and I realize why when I feel something hot and sticky on my hands, my arms, soaking into my clothes.

"Athena," I hiss, bringing her inside, slamming the door closed behind us, flicking the lock.

Her eyes are barely open. "Cupcake," she corrects on a rasp.

My heart squeezes.

Christ. This fucking woman.

I love her so goddamned much.

"I need to get you to the hospital," I growl. "Need to call an ambulance."

Her lids peel back in a flash, hand suddenly gripping my wrist. "No ambulance. No hospital."

"You're bleeding, cupcake," I say, bringing her into the bathroom, setting her gently on the counter. I know I have a first aid kit under the sink, so I bend down, open the cabinet, reach for the plastic-sided container—

"Not just bleeding," she forces out through rapid—and painful-sounding—exhalations. "Shot."

I freeze, fingers around the first aid kit. "What did you say?"

But I don't get the chance to hear the answer to my question.

Because now she's collapsing for real.

And when I catch her this time—barely managing to stop her from cracking her head on the marble countertop—a blood-soaked photograph falls out of her pocket, flutters to the ground.

I look down…

And see that it's Angela Rosseau.

Chrissy's, mom. Jean-Michel's ex. And the woman who's currently making big trouble for him.

What the actual fuck?

"Cam—" Athena's fingers wrap weakly around my wrist, and I tear my eyes from the photograph.

"Hold on, baby," I say as I open the first aid kit, grabbing a package of gauze, tearing the wrapper open with my teeth. "I need to get you to the hospital." I press it against her side, hate the cry of pain she gives in response. "You're—"

"No hospital." Another light squeeze on my wrist as she battles with staying conscious. "Lex is already on his way."

I frown. "He's not even in town."

"Flew in yesterday," she grunts when I press harder, her blood already seeping through the gauze. "Help with." She hisses out a breath. "Case. Warehouse. Got them."

"I don't care. You—"

POUND. POUND. POUND!
She smiles weakly. "See? Lex."
And then she passes out.

CHAPTER THIRTY-TWO

Ats

"Wʜᴀᴛ ᴛʜᴇ ꜰᴜᴄᴋ did you think you were doing going in there alone?"

I grit my teeth together, glaring at Lex as I hold still and allow the doctor to check her handiwork on my gunshot wound. "I didn't go in alone," I remind him.

He glares. "Fine. Didn't go *in* alone, just stayed and did stupid shit after Sandra called it off."

That I can't argue with.

I want to, just because he's yelling at me.

But he's not wrong.

We staked out the warehouse all night, looking for an opening, but it was too dangerous. Not enough agents. Not a clear line of sight. Not the right time.

So, Sandra called it off.

Regroup.

Refocus.

Come back out and try again.

I'd been on board with that—up until I started slipping away to my car and saw the box truck pull in.

And the girls, scared and clinging to each other, dressed… well, dressed like they were going to be auctioned off, were being loaded into the back.

I knew if they were locked in, driven off…

We would never find them again.

I close my eyes, exhale, then wince as the doctor finishes with the wound at my side.

"Rest for minimum of four weeks," she tells me, tugging my gown back down and the blanket back up. She peels off her gloves and tosses them into the trash before typing something on the computer parked next to the bed. "Longer if you push it," she adds, giving me a look that communicates she knows exactly how I feel about someone ordering me to rest. "It's not serious—"

Lex makes a sound of protest, but she just keeps her eyes on mine, holding my gaze.

"It's not serious," she says again, "but you can sure as hell make it become that way."

I grind my back teeth together, but I get the message loud and clear, so I nod.

She nods in return then steps back to the computer. Her fingers fly across the keyboard for several moments.

Moments that Lex spends sighing and shifting next to me, clearly impatient for me to explain exactly what the fuck-all I'd been thinking going into the warehouse alone.

I *hadn't* been thinking.

I'd been reacting.

Which is why I'm lying here with four weeks of rest ahead of me, listening to a doctor play typewriter on an industrial keyboard as my best friend in the entire world gets more pissed at me by the moment.

Stupid as hell.

So much of the last week is stupid as hell.

But that's a problem for tomorrow me—when the drugs wear off.

The doc pushes in the keyboard, says, "I'll send the nurse in with your discharge instructions."

"Thanks," I mutter.

She nods. "Be careful out there."

"Always am."

Lies.

Something else she sees, though she doesn't call me on it. She just flicks up her brows, glances at Lex, and then slips out into the hallway.

Of the hospital.

I should have gone home, should have taken care of it myself, but…

Cam.

I had needed *Cam.*

And Lex.

My family.

Because…I was scared and in love and miserable and alone and—

Even *if* the stubborn fucks had called an ambulance—though I told them both not too because I was fine—and I've now spent the last hours getting patched up in the emergency department when a couple of butterfly bandages and some gauze would have done the job…I can't be mad.

I love them.

And I need them.

And—

"*Why* the fuck—"

I hold my hand up, barely able to bite back the wince— because, yup, the good drugs are starting to wear off now. But I *do* manage it and say, "It was dumb as hell. I know that. *You* know that. But the girls were getting ready to be shipped out and the *oldest* one is sixteen." I drop my hand to my side, and I grimace, though at least Lex is doing the same. "The *oldest*," I repeat. "I couldn't—"

He exhales and shoves a hand through his hair, and I know I've won, at least a little.

He wouldn't have been able to walk away either.

"You're lucky you're not fucking dead, Attie."

I let the nickname slide—just this time. Because he's right. And because Cam's gotten me used to Athena, to Cupcake. To accepting that I'm not what my parents tried to make me.

No, *I've* been doing that too.

"I know," I whisper.

I was scared out of my mind, huddled in the corner of the warehouse, clinging to the shadows, participating in an illegal firefight in a very not nice part of town, waiting for that sixteen-year-old girl—the only one old enough to know how to drive the van I'd found and loaded the other girls into—to get far enough away for me to make a break for my car parked several blocks over.

The men guarding the warehouse weren't happy about losing their merchandise nor about my interference—

The through-and-through on my side is more than enough proof of that.

"But I had to," I mutter.

Lex sighs again and sinks down into the chair next to me, his thundercloud of anger evaporating like valley fog on a hot summer day. "I know." A beat as he takes my hand. "But it was still fucking stupid."

I want to laugh, but because that'll fucking hurt, I just shake my head. "Yeah," I say quietly, "it was."

His fingers wrap around mine. "The girls are safe. They drove straight to the office and Connie met them."

My throat goes tight, and part of me hates that my eyes start stinging, but I manage, "Great."

A squeeze. "You did good, kid."

I laugh weakly. "That's *my* line to say after you do something stupid and somehow survive."

He scowls, but only for a second before going back to teasing, "You always have all the good ones." His big shoulder lifts then drops. "So, I gotta take what I can."

I open my mouth to give him another one, but I don't get to release my snark because the nurse walks in then, and he starts briskly giving me my discharge instructions.

It's all the usual stuff—keep the wounds clean, coming back if I spike a fever, staying on top of my pain medicine and antibiotics.

And making sure I rest.

Ugh. The idea of rest when we're this close, when I need to talk to Jean-Michel, when we need to put this thing to bed…

Painful.

But something I don't have time to ruminate on because the next hour is filled with getting dressed in some old scrubs and signing paperwork and being wheeled out to his rental car.

Cam isn't outside, even though I scan the shadows for him.

And I don't have the heart to ask where he is.

He called me baby.

But he asked for space.

He loves me.

But might not be sure it's enough.

"Don't bleed in this one," Lex mutters as he buckles me in. "I didn't buy the insurance."

I snort then grit my teeth together at the bolt of pain. "Hilarious."

"I thought so." He slams my door, rounds the hood, and gets in the driver's seat, carefully navigating us away from the hospital and onto the freeway.

I can't lie.

The fatigue catches up with me and pretty soon my eyes are sliding closed and I'm dozing off and—

I stir when the car comes to a halt, slowly peeling my eyes open, and then gaping at my former partner.

Because Lex hasn't driven me home.

He's taken me to Cam's house.

My teeth click together. "Lex—"

"Shut it," he snaps, jabbing a finger in my direction. "I know there's something going on between you two."

"There's—"

"Don't lie to me. He was out of his mind. And you've spent the last week sounding—and now that I'm here—*looking* like a puppy that's been kicked." He nods to the house. "So you're staying here until it's fixed."

Only, what if Cam doesn't want to fix it?

"And by the way," Lex says, turning off the ignition and swiveling in his seat to fix me in place with a narrow-eyed glare. "I had Cam drop your car at the bio-hazard cleaners, so deal with being here until you both fix it…or I decide you're ready to have your keys back."

"Seriously?" I snap. "I'm an adult, you know."

"I know. And?"

And…

What if Cam doesn't want me here and I need to GTFO?

"It's full of blood, Ats"—he jabs at the button to unlatch his seat belt—"same as Cam's entryway and bathroom were when I found you."

Guilt slices through my middle, but I hold tight to the anger and grit out, "I could have cleaned it up."

He sniffs. "When you can't even get your T-shirt on by yourself?"

I growl.

Then wince.

Both because it hurts and because he's right—I needed his help to get dressed in the hospital.

Ugh.

And both of which he clearly sees.

He rolls his eyes and unfolds himself out of the car, leaving me with a statement that steals my words almost as effectively as the pain radiating through my insides.

"Fix it, Ats," he murmurs. "Find a way to fix it before it's too late. Otherwise"—his eyes bore into mine—"you'll regret it forever."

CHAPTER THIRTY-THREE

Cam

I'M SITTING on the couch after scrubbing her blood off the floor, after bleaching the shit out of several loads of laundry, and after forcing myself to not lose my cool, get in my car, and force my way into Athena's hospital room.

She didn't need a confrontation.

She needed care.

So, I did what I could—I dropped her car to get cleaned, grabbed Cookie from her house so he'd be looked after, and I defrosted some cinnamon rolls.

"Meow?"

Okay, so maybe I picked up Cookie so I would have someone to pass the time with, would have an excuse to go back and see her.

To get on my knees and grovel like I should have in her kitchen a week ago.

"It's okay, buddy," I tell him, stroking my fingers through his fur, reassuring both him and myself because we've both been sitting in my living room for hours waiting for Lex to tell me she's on her way home.

Not sleeping.

In limbo.

Waiting for my chance to drive back over to her house and fix this.

You're not good enough. Will never be good enough. You can't even give her kids.

"Fuck off," I whisper, grinding my teeth together.

"Meow?"

I cuddle Cookie close. "Not you, bud. Me. My brain. My idiotic thoughts." I sigh. "Maybe I won't ever feel good enough," I tell the voice in my head. "Maybe I won't ever feel good enough on the ice or off it. Maybe I can't give her everything she wants, but—"

"Maybe she doesn't need everything you think she wants."

Stilling at the voice, I lurch up from the couch and see Athena hobbling into the room, Lex hovering at her side, ready to help, and—

I stop thinking so fucking hard.

I move to her in a rush. "I'm so fucking sorry, cupcake. I-I—"

"Was in your head again?" she asks softly.

You're not good enough.

The voice is there, loud and blaring, but for the first time since I walked into her kitchen a week ago, I'm able to bat it away, able to focus on the woman I love.

"I'm sorry," I say, gently—oh so fucking *gently*—cupping her jaw. "I hurt you and I was out of my mind, but that's no excuse. I know you wouldn't—"

Her eyes slide closed, and she exhales. Then winces.

Dammit.

She's hurting.

"Come on," I say, carefully looping my arm around her shoulders, drawing her to the couch and helping her sit down.

Distantly, I hear the front door click closed, know that Lex is leaving.

Same as I know my family will have a full report in

minutes…and he'll want an explanation at some point—and a promise that I won't fuck up again.

You're not good enough.

It's only a whisper now, and I slam it down, focus on what's more important.

"Meow." Cookie hops onto the couch, sniff's at Athena's side then settles in *oh so carefully.*

Such a good cat.

Such a good *woman.*

I grind my teeth together.

I am *not* going to fuck this up again.

"Hi, baby," she murmurs, stroking him carefully. Then she looks up at me. "I was coming over. Last night," she adds when I feel my brow furrow. "Before I got that call that we were a go for the warehouse, and before I likely torpedoed my career."

I take her hand. "It shouldn't have been necessary. I've been being a coward all week, knowing I need to make the first move, but unable to shake the voices in my head."

"You're not perfect, Cam."

I snort. "Clearly."

"And neither am I." Her mouth curves in a ghost of a smile. "It was destined for one of us to fuck up sooner rather than later. The space I can understand." Her smile fades. "But as the week went on, I thought…"

My stomach churns. "Thought what?"

"Thought the reality of being with me was too much."

"Fuck," I hiss, jumping to my feet and pacing away. "Fuck, baby," I say turning back and dropping to my knees in front of her, needing her to see me, to see the truth in my eyes. "I'm so sorry. It wasn't you at all. I…I loved you for so long and being with you is so much more than I could have hoped for. When I saw the case, heard that Jean-Michel asked for help solving my bullshit…"

I close my eyes, grit my teeth together, bat down the humiliation.

"You doing this—*us*—for work was the only thing that made sense. It couldn't be me, clearly, I'm not good enough. I can't give you kids, can't carry the team, can't even relationship right, and I know that's not all I am, not the logical train of thought but—"

"Old habits die hard."

I nod. "But, cupcake, you came to me. You were hurting and fucking shot and you came here and knew I'd have you and—"

My eyes sting. My voice breaks.

"Seeing you like that, I knew—fucking *knew*—that I could lose you in an instant. Not just because of your job, but an accident, an illness, *life,* and that would be terrible. But what would be worse?" I hold her eyes. "Losing you because I was too much of a coward to stop and think, because it was easier to assume, easier to accept the bullshit in my head? Now that would *kill* me."

You're not good enough.

It's barely audible, so soft the words are almost garbled.

"I'm going to talk to someone," I say softly. "Going to work with a therapist to break these habits, to talk through my injury, to make sure I have the coping skills I need to make sure I never —fucking *never*—do this shit to you again."

"Honey," she whispers. "It's not just you. I...well, I have plenty of baggage."

Smiling, I gently cup her cheek. "So we'll figure out how to check that shit together. Because you're too important to me to just let you go."

A tear clings to her lashes, slides down her cheek. "I blocked her," she whispers.

My heart squeezes, pride for her filling me to bursting. I take her hand, squeeze lightly. "Tell me."

So, she does.

About the messages and finally having enough. About the going back into the warehouse after the raid was called off.

About saving the girls even as she got herself into a sticky situation.

"I am so fucking proud of you," I whisper as I cup her face in my hands, "but if you ever do that again—"

She winces, covering my hands with her own. "Believe me," she whispers. "I know. And Lex read me the riot act already." Another wince. "Along with Sandra."

"And now Jean-Michel is going to."

We both blink and turn to the side, seeing that the man in question is standing in the hall, his eyes fixed on us.

"You called," he says.

"Two days ago," Athena counters.

"I was in France."

"Takes a hot minute to fuel up the jet," Lex quips as he follows Jean-Michel into the room.

"Seriously?" I ask both of them. "Have you been listening the whole time?"

Lex has the good sense to look chagrined. "Not the *whole* time."

I sit back on my heels, rub at my temple, at the throb forming there. "Go away, the both of you. Athena needs rest."

Steel in my friend's, my *brother's* eyes. "I think we need to have a talk first."

"You think you could tell me anything I haven't already told myself that will get this bullshit out of my head for once and for all?" I exhale, table my anger, knowing he's just concerned. "It's not that easy and you know it."

Lex's face smooths out and Jean-Michel steps closer, but I barely process that because Athena's talking. "Yup," she quips. "Lay it on us. The magic bullet that will solve all our problems."

Lex scowls. "I—" But he doesn't finish the sentence.

"Exactly," she says. "You can't. But considering for you it was finding Frankie"—she takes my hands—"and considering that *we've* found each other, I think we're off to a good start."

He scowls. "I don't want either of you to think you're not good—"

"You can't control our thoughts," I say quietly. "Half the time I can't control my *own* thoughts."

"Here."

I blink, watch as Jean-Michel walks over to us, handing us both business cards.

"What's this, JM?" Athena asks quietly.

His face is gentle when he looks at her, but his words are gruff. "She'll help you find someone to talk to."

I still, shame threatening to well up.

Then he adds, "I know because she helped me."

Even as I'm processing that—and how it settles the shame—any sign of soft disappears from Jean-Michel's face, a flickering muscle appearing in his jaw. "Now, three things—one, why did you tell me to get my ass home two days ago; two, why are you sitting on this fucking couch with a bullet wound in your side; and three, why the *fuck* is there a bloodied picture of my ex-wife on Cam's counter?"

CHAPTER THIRTY-FOUR

Athena

I HAVE the great pleasure to be sitting in the office the next week when Peter Auclair strolls into the practice facility, thinking he's at the top of the world.

The asshole is whistling for fuck's sake.

By all intents and purposes, the FBI's backed off since my escapades at the warehouse.

The Lyons think they're in the clear.

But in *reality*, we've shifted our investigation to the connection between Jean-Michel's ex-wife—the woman who's reappeared from the shadows to create chaos for the grumpy silver fox and his various businesses—and the Lyons.

And it's bigger than anything we ever thought possible.

It'll take time to build the case, of course, but today…

We have the great pleasure of witnessing the arrest of one Peter Auclair…after, of course, Jean-Michel fires him for gambling on Eagles games.

The league's commissioner already knows what's going down and is prepared to issue a lifetime ban.

Fucking brilliant.

The only downside is that I have to watch it go down from my chair in the corner of the Peter's office.

Four weeks of rest.

Jesus Christ.

I know I only have myself to blame, same as I know that I'm lucky to still have my job—and to have only received a written warning—for my shenanigans at the warehouse.

I still say it's worth it.

Especially, when Connie told me that the girls have been reunited with their families, families she personally vetted and ensured were safe.

Maybe they're not perfect, and I'm definitely going to be keeping an eye on them.

Going to make sure they're safe.

When I can get out of bed, that is.

In…three more weeks.

"Tommy would have loved this," Lex murmurs from where he's propping up the wall next to me. Sandra issued him the professional courtesy because—in her words—*"he saved your dumb ass by calling an ambulance."*

Not serious.

It was a very *not serious* bullet wound.

Why do I have to keep reminding everyone of that fact?

But even as I think that, I'm smothering my smile. I know it's bullshit, know I got lucky, know that…I was wrong before. There's another downside of today.

Yes, we've nailed Peter Auclair, and so his toxic presence won't be dragging down the Eagles organization any longer, but he wasn't the one who pulled the trigger.

He wasn't the one who killed Tommy last year.

That's still an open case I'm determined to solve. No, not just *determined*.

I'm *going* to solve it.

I exhale, feel my stitches protest, but it's getting better. A couple more days and they'll be out, and then I'll spend a few more weeks on desk duty.

Now if I can just find a way to have sex with Cam and *not* break the rest edict, my life will be pretty fucking perfect.

Because I have the feeling we're going to want to celebrate tonight.

I watch via the camera feed we set up as Peter whistles his way inside, jauntily swiping his badge and meandering down the hall, likely looking for someone to bully—

For Cam.

Who's waiting just outside his office door.

We follow the feed, switching cameras until Peter spots Cam and picks up his pace, a shark in the water who's smelled blood.

I narrow my eyes, know that Cam's got this.

That he *needs* this.

But I still want to quietly dispose of Peter Auclair.

"Hey, Coach," I hear Cam say as Peter opens his mouth, beating the asshole to the punch and tilting his head toward the office. "Got a second?"

A second to enter the office and be arrested by federal agents.

"No," Peter snaps, affecting a toddler prepared to tantrum, clearly upset that his fun has been ruined. "I'm busy. Go away."

"Nope," Cam tells him cheerfully. "I won't." He reaches for the door handle, pushes the metal panel inward and clamps his hand onto Peter's shoulder, guiding him roughly inside. "Enjoy jail, motherfucker," he says as my coworkers surround him. "Also"—he crouches in front of Auclair, holds his gaze—"you're an asshole."

Then he's smiling as he crosses over to me and we watch as Peter is frog-marched out. When the fucker is gone, Cam touch my shoulder gently. "Good, cupcake?"

I nod, but I know that he sees I'm lying—oh, I'm positively gleeful that Peter's getting his comeuppance—but I feel the fatigue sweeping in.

Rest.

Fucking rest—I hate that I need it.

"Lex?" he says quietly and my former partner glances over at us. "Taking her home."

Lex nods. "You pull up the car, I'll walk her out, load her up."

"I'm not a package to be chucked in the back of the car," I grumble after Cam disappears down the hall and Lex walks my weak and tired ass out to the parking lot.

"I didn't say I'd *chuck* you in." Amusement in Lex's voice. "I'll set you carefully into the passenger's seat. Hell, I'll even throw in free buckling."

I glare at him, but it's taking most of my energy to walk the thirty feet down the hall.

"I second what Cam said," he murmurs as we reach the door to the outside.

"About taking me home?" I ask, or well, grumble. "I know I've reach my limit. I don't need two men to tell me what to do."

He touches my cheek. "About being proud of how far you've come."

I still, heart squeezing hard.

"I love you, Ats," he says roughly, "and even though I already consider you my sister, I love that you'll be even more deeply ensnared into the Jacksons now that you're with Cam."

My eyes sting, but my mouth quirks up. "No spiel about being good enough for your little brother?"

He grins, but his tone is serious when he says, "No one will ever be good enough for you." He leans in and kisses the top of my head. "But Cam's as close to that as possible."

"It's your fault, you know?" I manage to ask lightly, desperately blinking back tears.

"What is?"

"That my heart isn't frozen in ice any longer."

"*Ats,*" he rasps.

"You chipped away at the shields."

His throat works and then he hugs me carefully. "I took a blowtorch to them is more like it."

"Though," I say, knowing we need to lighten the mood before I turn into a puddle of tears, "I guess the *real* difference were Martha's cinnamon rolls."

He laughs then leads me over to where Cam has parked. "I think hearing that would make her day."

"I know," I say but then my focus is diverted.

Because my heart is now standing in front of me, held safe and protected and…in Cam's hands.

Lex gives him a noogie. "Love you, kid."

"Ugh." He bats him away then smiles. "Love you too—even though you're a pain in my ass."

"Rude."

But then Cam is helping me fold into the seat, and he's saying goodbye to Lex, who says that we'll see him later for lunch before he flies home.

And we're heading home.

After my nap, with Cookie by my side, we hang with Lex. And after my second nap—I'm resting, okay?—he hands me my laptop and a warm cinnamon roll.

And after *that* we spend a perfect evening killing orcs.

It's not what I expected, or even what I dreamed of.

And it's not perfect, but that's okay.

Because I know that Cam and I are going to make sure it's perfect for *us*.

With cinnamon rolls and whisky and a cat who makes biscuits on my face.

And each other.

That's the most important part.

EPILOGUE

Athena, Two Months Later

"You know," I say as I watch my man shrug into a suit jacket that should be sin personified, "you never did tell me why you call me cupcake."

He grins as he straightens his tie. "No," I say, "I didn't."

I prop my hands beneath my chin, holding still as Cookie crawls up my back, nuzzling at my hair. "Meow," he croons, settling in for his mid-mid-*mid* afternoon nap.

"Are you *going* to?" I prompt when he doesn't go on.

His grin widens as he comes to the bed and puts on his shoes. "I wasn't planning on it."

I swat at him, disturbing Cookie, who gives me a baleful look before curling up against my side.

"Meow," he warns.

"Cam," *I* warn.

He leans down and kisses my temple. "You're beautiful," he says simply.

Those two words never fail to send my heart skittering and today is no exception. "Honey," I whisper.

"That's the truth"—he cups my jaw, slants his mouth over mine for a long, drugging kiss—"*and* the explanation."

He stands and starts gathering his stuff for the game, and I'm so in the haze of his pleasurable distraction that it takes me a minute to process his words. "What do you mean, it's the explanation?"

His lips twitch as he slings his messenger bag over his shoulder then holds his hand out. "I mean what I said."

I lace my fingers through his, let him draw me from the room.

And along the hall.

And down the stairs.

And…

Into the kitchen.

"Don't you have to go to the game?" I ask when he all but drags me to the fridge. Cam has a routine on game days and I know this isn't his snack time.

"Yup," he says, dropping my hand as he tugs open the door, reaches in, pulls out a small blue bakery box emblazoned with *Molly's* on the front, and sets it in my hands.

"Um…" I whisper.

He carefully opens the lid.

My heart catches—and my stomach growls—at the sight of the cupcakes we picked up earlier today. It's the first game of the season and the Eagles are playing at home.

I'm watching. Cam is going to kick ass.

And then we're going to celebrate by eating cupcakes and killing orcs.

"Aren't we saving these for later?" I ask quietly.

"We were," he says, reaching in and pulling out the cupcake I'd picked—a beautiful chocolate with vanilla buttercream concoction. A delicate swirl of frosting, glittering sprinkles, the barest touch of gold leaf.

It's gorgeous.

I couldn't take my eyes off it.

And Cam noticed—because of course he did—buying it and four others for us—

"Hey!"

But he's already moving to the counter, snagging a plate, reaching for a knife.

"What are you—?"

"You're beautiful," he says, pointing to the dessert. "Exquisite, just like these cupcakes from Molly's." His mouth turns up. "I remember the first time I saw one, it reminded me of you—stunning, untouchable, and yet I couldn't stop myself from taking it home and making it mine."

"Cam," I murmur, heart skipping a beat.

"But I couldn't see the whole picture just from looking at the outside. I was distracted by the beauty, the sparkles, the perfectly piped frosting." He lifts the knife and cuts carefully through the cupcake. "I was preoccupied by what I saw, baby. By what I thought I felt, and it wasn't until I was able to see beyond all of that—"

He pulls the two sides apart and I gasp.

"—and glimpse the beauty inside, that I truly understood, that I truly *saw.*"

My heart is pounding. "Honey," I whisper, eyes burning, tears gathering.

Because—

"You were always that cupcake, something beautiful I thought I knew, but—"

He reaches into the layers of cake and filling and jam, and pulls out something that has my pulse skittering through my veins.

"—the inside is so much more awe-inspiring. You, baby. *You're* awe-inspiring and mine and I don't ever want to let you go. You're strong and capable and smart. Funny and sweet and *mine.* You're my protector, my partner, my *future.*"

I'm crying now but can't seem to stop.

Not when I've never felt more loved, more seen.

More *me.*

"And so," he says, holding up the ring he extracted. "With all of that being said, my beautiful cupcake, the woman who owns my heart and soul, will you marry me?"

I move to him, tears dripping down my cheeks, love for this man filling me to bursting, and know that I'm the luckiest woman on the planet as I say,

"Only if you throw in the Sex Cave."

Because I'm me.

But he gets that.

So, his mouth curves.

And his arms band around me.

And he leans close to whisper in my ear,

"Done."

And it turns out that nobody cares all that much if you show up late to opening night…

Especially when you show off the big ass diamond on your ring finger.

And your brand new hot hockey hunk of a fiancé.

Hudson

I'm fucked I realize as I stare up at the tiny spitfire of a woman.

Who's lecturing me.

In a lilting voice that I can't help but get lost in the melody of.

"…and I really need you to take some time to focus on this new system," she saying, gesturing at an iPad. "I know it's new and it's tough to make these changes, but this will make it much easier for us to mobilize your speed and strength."

She pauses.

And I realize that I'm staring.

That I'm so caught up in the beauty of her, I haven't processed she's expecting an answer.

"Got it," I manage to rasp out.

She nods then rounds the desk and moves to the door of her office, pulling it open so I can see the hallway beyond.

Her office.

The new head coach of the Eagles, Diana Connors.

The first female head coach in the league.

And the object of my fantasies since she first showed up at training camp.

"I'll see you out on the ice," she says in that quiet, sure, *melodic* voice.

And…

I'm staring again.

Committing every freckle, every eyelash to memory.

Obsessed.

She clears her throat, brow furrowing. "Hudson?" she asks quietly. "Is everything okay?"

I nod. "Sorry," I mutter, shoving to my feet, and moving to the door, feeling like a fucking lumbering giant as I get close to her. "Just tired," I add by way of explanation. "I'll be good by practice though."

Her expression smooths. "Okay, Huddy," she says. "I'll let you get dressed."

That does something to me.

No, not *something*.

Her soft voice calling me my nickname wraps invisible fingers around my cock and strokes.

Stupid.

I bob my head at her and start to step into the hall.

"Huddy?"

I stop, glance over my shoulder.

She opens her mouth.

But I never do hear her question…

Because that moment, the world starts violently shaking.

———

THANK YOU FOR READING! I hope you loved Athena and Cam's love story as much as I enjoyed writing it! The next full-length book in the Eagles Hockey series is LUCKY LACES. **I thought I had my whole life figured out...and then the world started shaking.**

CLICK HERE TO READ LUCKY LACES NOW>

AND IN THE MEANTIME, don't miss more Eagles hockey with the novella, LOADED LACES. **Every wonder what happens when you're in the locker room and ask a sexy hockey player a loaded question? Well...I'm about to find out.**

CLICK HERE TO READ LOADED LACES NOW>

———

Want a sneak peek into Jean-Michel's book, BOTTLES AND BLADES. **He's ruthless and goes after what he wants. And he's decided...That's me.**
Read on below!
CLICK HERE TO READ BOTTLES AND BLADES NOW>

Tiff

"YOUR TOTAL IS $23.26," the cashier says, tapping on the register's keyboard, the computer screen above it changing as rapidly as her fingers move.

Clickity-click. Clickity-click. Clickity-click.

She pauses, glances up.

But not at me.

At the man she's currently checking out, the man just in front of me. The man who reacts after a brief moment, jerking as though jarred from his thoughts and reaching into his pocket.

He's wearing a pair of jeans stained with so much dirt that I pity his washing machine, and his tee isn't much better, filthy and sweat-covered, plastered against a broad, well-muscled chest.

His forearms and hands are stained with something dark.

Clearly coming from some sort of hard, physical work, and on a day like today, summer clinging to the edges of a sunny spring afternoon, I envy him.

Not that I don't love my job—I'm a nanny, and my charge is awesome, and I love that it gives me the freedom to pursue my degree.

But sometimes I wouldn't mind playing hooky and getting out on one of the many trails around us on this side of the Bay, all rolling green hills and old-growth oaks and spring wildflowers.

"Sir?"

I blink, realize that while I've been daydreaming about poppies and blue lupines, the man in front of me has been searching his pockets.

And coming up empty.

"Your total is $23.26," the cashier repeats, a little sharper now.

"Right," the man says, patting his pockets in turn. "Just give me a second. I know my wallet—"

"If you can't pay, I'm going to have to ask you step aside and let the others behind you have their turn." Her tone is brusque and cold and—

Filled with disdain.

It slices through me, even though it's not directed at me.

Because I've lived that life.

Because even today, I calculated my own spread on the conveyor belt, sitting behind the plastic divider, to a precise degree. I know that I have exactly the amount in my account to cover my food for the week.

Food and tuition. Medical debts and gas.

All of my expenses carefully worked out.

The man keeps searching. "I know I have—"

Someone sighs behind me—a sharp irritated sound that zips through the air, stinging as it flies by me.

The man looks up, mid pocket-pat, and I almost gasp at the startling blue of his eyes.

They're as bright as the cloudless sky outside the store and filled with embarrassment that has my heart squeezing.

"If you'll just give me a moment," he murmurs, eyes narrowing as they drift behind me, presumably toward the impatient sigher and the line that's growing by the moment. "I have—"

The cashier starts tapping on her keyboard again, this time angrily. "I'll have to cancel the transaction, sir."

It's the condescension in her tone that unsticks me.

I double tap the side of my cell, take a step toward the man with the dirt marring his strong chin, clinging to the salt and pepper beard on his jaw, his cheeks. I slip between his strong, obviously hardworking body and the payment kiosk, avoiding those bright blue eyes as I say, "I've got it."

That brilliant cerulean gaze comes to mine. "No, that's—"

But I'm already waving my phone at the machine, and it doesn't so much as have to make contact to solve this problem.

Bleep-beep.

And it's done.

"There," I say softly, giving him a small smile. "Enjoy your meal."

His expression…

Well, I'm not sure I can discern the flurry of emotions—annoyance and surprise and embarrassment and…

Gratitude.

"Thank you," he says softly, snagging the sandwich, soda, and bag of chips from the counter.

"No worries," I reply, turning back to the cashier, taking the receipt she passes over.

He waits there for a moment, big body still, eyes on me, so I turn and hold it out to him.

"Did you need this?" I ask, careful to not get lost in his eyes, careful to not notice how handsome he is, all strong muscles and brutal features and those gorgeous blue irises.

"No," he says.

But doesn't move.

Just stares at me like I'm a puzzle to be solved.

And well…no puzzle here.

Just a woman who's barely holding her life together.

"Right, okay." I nibble at the corner of my mouth. "You have a good day."

Another hesitation from the big man next to me.

"You're all paid, sir," the cashier snaps as she starts scanning my items. "You can go now."

I see him stiffen out of the corner of my eye, but he doesn't snap back, and…he doesn't linger.

Just gives a slight nod and walks away.

Some part of me is disappointed.

The rest…is relieved.

Beep. Beep. Beep. Beep—

"Wait," I tell the cashier, as she reaches for the bottle of wine. It's a discount brand, but I'll have to do without it after that $23.26. "I'll pass on the wine," I say softly.

Her eyes come to mine and she rolls hers, silently setting it to the side before reaching for the next item.

A block of cheese.

"And that too," I murmur, doing some mental math. "And the bread," I add when she puts that aside, starts to scan.

More eye rolls, but my math proves to be on point because by the time she finishes scanning—minus the cheese and bread and wine—I have enough left in my account to cover everything else.

I click the button on the side of my phone.

Do another wave of my cell, hear that bleep-beep.

And ignore the surly cashier as I bag my items, gather up my receipt, and head out of the store.

I'm putting my bags into my trunk when I feel a presence behind me.

I close the lid, spin around, and—

See the man from the store standing there, eyes flashing, body big and broad and giving more than a few Daddy vibes.

My heart skips a beat.

Warmth blooms in my belly.

Lower.

He's too old for me.

But my mind is running away with itself anyway.

"Can I help you—?" I begin.

"Come with me," he mutters.

Before I can protest, he wraps his fingers around my arm.

And drags me away from my car.

————

Hate missing Elise's new releases? Love contests, exclusive excerpts and giveaways?
Then signup for Elise's newsletter here!
www.elisefaber.com/newsletter

————

If you enjoy my series, considering supporting me on PATREON! Get access to early releases, bonus content, character art, audiobooks, and much more!
CLICK HERE TO SUPPORT ME>

————

And join Elise's fan group, the Fabinators (https://www.facebook.com/groups/fabinators) for insider information, sneak peaks at new releases, and fun freebies! Hope to see you there!

————

EAGLES HOCKEY SERIES

Eagles Hockey Series (all stand alone)
Broken Laces
Lace 'em Up
Knotted Laces
Loaded Laces
Lucky Laces

Ballsy

Bewitched

Blowout

Breathe

Blazed

Sierra Hockey Series

Over the Line

Caught from Behind

On the Fly

The Big Skate

Rush Hockey Trilogy #1

Big Puck Energy

Filthy Puckboy

So Pucking Over It

Rush Hockey Trilogy #2

Love, Pucks, and Other Stories

All's Fair in Pucks and War

No Pucks Lost Between Us

Rush Hockey Novella

Puck and Make Up

Eagles Hockey Series (all stand alone)

Broken Laces

Lace 'em Up

Knotted Laces

Loaded Laces

Lucky Laces

Billionaire's Club **(all stand alone)**

Bad Night Stand

Bad Breakup

Bad Husband

Bad Hookup

Bad Divorce

Bad Fiancé

Bad Boyfriend

Bad Blind Date

Bad Wedding

Bad Engagement

Bad Bridesmaid

Bad Swipe

Bad Girlfriend

Bad Best Friend

Bad Rebound

Bad Romance

Bad Business

Bad Billionaire's Quickies

Love, Action, Camera **(all stand alone)**

Dotted Line

Action Shot

Close-Up

End Scene

Meet Cute

Love After Midnight **(all stand alone)**

Rum And Notes

Virgin Daiquiri

On The Rocks

Sex On The Seats

Life Sucks Series

Train Wreck

Hot Mess

Dumpster Fire

Clusterf*@k

FUBAR

Perfect Storm

Free Fall

Lost Cause

Roosevelt Ranch Series **(all stand alone, series complete)**

Disaster at Roosevelt Ranch

Heartbreak at Roosevelt Ranch

Collision at Roosevelt Ranch

Regret at Roosevelt Ranch

Desire at Roosevelt Ranch

Phoenix Series **(read in order)**

Phoenix Rising

Dark Phoenix

Phoenix Freed

Phoenix: LexTal Chronicles **(rereleasing soon, stand alone, Phoenix world)**

From Ashes

In Flames

To Smoke

KTS Series (all stand alone, series complete)

Riding The Edge

Crossing The Line

Leveling The Field

Scorching The Earth

Cocky Heroes World

Tattooed Troublemaker

www.ingramcontent.com/pod-product-compliance
Lightning Source LLC
Chambersburg PA
CBHW070642100726

ABOUT THE AUTHOR

USA Today bestselling author, Elise Faber, loves chocolate, Star Wars, Harry Potter, and hockey (the order depending on the day and how well her team — the Sharks! — are playing). She and her husband also play as much hockey as they can squeeze into their schedules, so much so that their typical date night is spent on the ice. Elise is the mom to two exuberant boys and lives in Northern California. Connect with her in her Facebook group, the Fabinators or find more information about her books at www.elisefaber.com.

facebook.com/elisefaberauthor

amazon.com/author/elisefaber

bookbub.com/profile/elise-faber

instagram.com/elisefaber

tiktok.com/@elisefaberauthor

goodreads.com/elisefaber